T0149456

# A Spiral of Time

Book One of the Born Crystal Series

K. V. Donato

# A SPIRAL OF TIME
## BOOK ONE OF THE BORN CRYSTAL SERIES

iUniverse books may be ordered through booksellers or by contacting:

iUniverse
1663 Liberty Drive
Bloomington, IN 47403
www.iuniverse.com
1-800-Authors (1-800-288-4677)

ISBN: 978-1-5320-3257-8 (sc)
ISBN: 978-1-5320-3256-1 (e)

Library of Congress Control Number: 2017915947

Print information available on the last page.

iUniverse rev. date: 10/30/2017

*I dedicate this book to my son,*
*with love.*

# *Acknowledgments*

My heart is filled with gratitude for the people who have made possible the writing of this novel, *A Spiral of Time*, the first of the *Born Crystal* series. Many thanks go to my family, husband and son, for their unfailing support.

Many thanks to the Publisher.

My special thanks go to the silent editors—Kathy, Walter, Jenni, Sally and Bronwyn, for their many hours of work behind the scenes, assisting me in the editing of this book. Many thanks also go to my critic team—Jan, Mariane, Ginger, Merelyn, Kerry, Megan, Kyle, Kayleen, Desley, Don, Rebecca, Aaron and Margot.

Every day I feel blessed to be surrounded by people who love me unconditionally.

# 1

## *The Past Comes Calling*

Deacon Rainer, a young man of twenty-two, yawned slowly while stretching his tanned arms across his strong, muscular frame. Grabbing a chainsaw and ladder out of the garden shed, Deacon carried them effortlessly across the backyard. It was eight o'clock in the morning and above Deacon, the sky was an endless blue with not a cloud in sight.

In the far corner of the yard stood an enormous old tree where hummingbirds kept up their insistent noise in the shade of its broad leaves. Hidden inside the twisted branches and creeping vines sat a weather-beaten tree house—a secret boyhood hideout Deacon's father had built a long time ago. This was a private place, where he and his best buddy Jett, spent hours dreaming about becoming soldiers and defending their country. Wanting to follow in his father's footsteps, Deacon smiled as he remembered persuading Jett to make a pledge with him all those years ago to join the military when they were old enough.

It was a beautiful morning and a perfect time to prune

trees Deacon thought, as he squinted into the rising sun and caught his breath. He narrowed his dark eyes, raising a hand to shield his handsome face. In front of Deacon, the luminous rays struck the tangled green mass hanging wildly over the old wooden structure. A few minutes later he put the ladder on level ground, propping it against the sturdy trunk. Taking his water bottle out of his pocket, Deacon took a few gulps of water before he climbed the ladder. When he reached the top, Deacon gave the chainsaw starter cord a powerful tug, and on the second attempt the motor roared to life.

What Deacon first thought would be a simple task, had some hidden dangers which soon made an impact. It was painstaking work for the most part, slicing tree limbs and pulling at matted vines, with little progress to show for all his effort.

Suddenly, a sharp crack sounded above Deacon's head. A large branch unexpectedly splintered and then fell, hitting him hard. This blow caused the ladder to slide out from under Deacon. The chainsaw fell from his hands as his body went sideways in the air. Deacon tumbled roughly to the ground amid branches and a jumble of leaves. The chainsaw, still spluttering, landing nearby tearing up the grass.

Time seemed to slow down and sounds were muffled as Deacon lay on the shredded foliage with one hand resting on his dark, wavy hair, his head throbbing painfully. A thin line of blood, mixed with sweat, trickled down the side of his square jaw.

A plume of dust quickly rose in the air, and smoky fumes curled around the chainsaw. Deacon sat up slowly, then rolled onto his left side and managed to switch off the motor. Through the haze and his blurred vision, Deacon glimpsed part of the white picket fence that hugged the curve of the property.

Yellow and orange flowers bordering the lawn, gave him an immediate impression that the grass around the fence was on fire. Deacon was certain there was a wooden bench somewhere nearby, but it was nearly impossible to find it. The bench seemed to be consumed by a woven mass of thick weeds engulfed in flames.

Deacon's vision flickered as he was partially blinded by the bright sunlight. Still in a daze, he staggered to his feet. Bending down, he grasped the handle of the chainsaw with clenched fingers. The grass was thick with fallen leaves, and the smell of fuel still lingered in the air.

It took Deacon several minutes to find the wooden stairs leading to the back porch. Releasing the chainsaw, Deacon let it fall heavily to the ground. It presented no danger now with the motor switched off. Then, clinging to the railing with both hands and struggling to stay upright, Deacon somehow managed to call out, "Mom! Are you there?"

Lucy, Deacon's mother, who was engrossed in reading a recipe book in the kitchen, looked up in alarm when she heard the cry for help. Lucy flung open the back door forcefully and shouted, "Stay where you are! I'm coming!" There was a rush of activity as Lucy ran along the back porch and bounded down the wooden steps. In a moment, she was at her son's side.

"Deacon!" Lucy said sharply, trying to get him to concentrate. The desperate questions then came tumbling out—"Are you all right? What happened? What did you do?"

Deacon nodded, staring blankly, thankful she'd heard his voice. He was vaguely aware they were then somehow stumbling up the porch steps together. Once inside the house, Lucy steered him in the direction of the living room, where he soon found himself sitting awkwardly on the sofa.

"Stay here, Deacon, and don't move!" Lucy ordered. "I'll get the first aid kit and some ice for that nasty bump." Lucy left the room, brushing back a wisp of chestnut hair that had escaped from behind her ear. As she hurried, Lucy let the hair fall before nervously twisting her ponytail into a tight knot at the nape of her neck.

Deacon carefully stretched his T-shirt up over his head and then bent down to unlace his shoes. He slowly let himself lie back on the sofa, sinking into the soft cushions and closing his eyes as if to sleep. Almost immediately, he sat upright again, startled by the sound of someone walking heavily up the front steps. Before he could grab his mother's attention, there was a shrill ring from the doorbell, followed by an urgent pounding on the front door.

"Who … is … it?" Deacon's question was slurred as the effects of his fall started to show.

A second brisk ring followed, with more insistent knocking. Obviously, whoever it was at the door was not going to go away.

"Okay! I can hear you!" Despite his head still swirling around from the fall, Deacon staggered to his feet and lurched over to the window. Peering through the lace curtains, he craned his neck to look out. The sight which met his eyes was one his mind told him was impossible.

Just then, a gust of cold wind rustled through the treetops, accompanied by a strange whispering-like sound. He held back the curtain with his hands raised, as if to enjoy the warmth of the sun on his face, but his look was not of pleasure but of deep shock.

Deacon could just make out the shape of a man through

the window. Surprisingly, the face was one he thought he recognized from the old family photographs on the mantelpiece. He lowered his hands, twisted around, then stumbled toward the front door.

Nothing could have prepared Deacon for the sight that greeted him as he opened the door on that Friday morning. Filtered sunlight created skittish shadows that drifted across the wooden veranda, while the cool wind still stirred the trees. Clouds had begun to appear in the sky. Deacon's jaw dropped at the sight of what seemed to be his long-dead father standing before him.

Stunned and still dazed from the fall, Deacon had a thousand questions rush through his head. Trying hard to disguise his deep feelings of uncertainty and fear, Deacon finally managed to ask with some strength, "*Dad*! I thought you …." The question remained unfinished and there was no answer.

Even though his heart was racing, his breathing heavy, and every muscle in his body tensed, Deacon managed to summon the courage to look directly at the man's face. The striking Italian features seemed to command respect, and Deacon instantly recognised a family resemblance to himself.

Powerfully built, the man in front of Deacon looked to be well over six feet tall. Short, curly black hair framed a filthy tanned face. Deep wrinkles creased the corners of his dark, bloodshot eyes.

Unable to speak, Deacon instead took in the sight of the torn combat uniform, streaked from top to bottom with bloodstains and mud, right down to the dirty military boots with their laces tied so tight. The soldier standing in front of Deacon was certainly not dressed for a parade.

In an instant that seemed like madness, Deacon felt the sudden urge to reach out and touch the eerie figure, who reminded him of an actor from a war movie that Deacon had recently seen. A tingling sensation momentarily prickled the back of Deacon's neck. Blinking hard, he rubbed his eyes as if to make the person disappear.

The man began whispering in low, husky tones, and everything else around Deacon started to fade from sight. His voice was touched with a deep vibration that Deacon hadn't heard since childhood.

Another cold squall momentarily swept across the veranda. Deacon remained openmouthed, but now locked eyes with this person he knew instinctively to be his father, and tried to listen intently to what was being said.

"Deacon, I know this situation must be scaring you, but I want to assure you that you will come to no harm from me. I have little doubt that the family story you were told, said I was reported killed on active service when you were very young. Don't ask me by what means or through what power, but somehow I have found my way back to this place and into your presence, so I can deliver a critically important message.

"What I am about to tell you is based on the single truth that, across the fabric of the cosmos, all life forms are linked together in some way.

"Because of this truth, I need you to understand that this part of the universe we call the solar system, has become the realm of chaos.

"Twelve years ago, when you were just ten, I witnessed the passage toward the sun of what was an alien spacecraft moving outside the Earth's atmosphere. The first planet to be conquered by the dark force travelling in this vessel was Mercury. Then, the planet Venus suffered a horrendous invasion that altered it forever. Thousands of Venus's inhabitants were killed, but a small group of them did manage to escape being slaughtered when they were taken prisoner by a malicious warlord, known as Obsidian. Forcibly removed from their planet, these survivors of the conflict faced death or worse."

Deacon suddenly took a step back and leaned against the doorframe, feeling utterly confused. His father continued with the story, the words flowing like a song with a comforting beat, but with their meaning almost overwhelming Deacon completely.

"Deacon, my time here is short. You need to know that soon you and Jett will be called on to undertake a quest, which will be crucial for order to be restored amongst the planets. A Native American woman will guide you on this quest, providing you and Jett with the knowledge and wisdom necessary for you to succeed.

"What you will be asked to do, is to find the Sacred Keeper, a mysterious red creature, who is the guardian of certain small beings, described in many languages as the Crystals. The future of these Crystals depends on the Sacred Keeper, so when the call comes, you and Jett must find the Sacred Keeper and carry out the task given to you.

"None of this has a certain outcome, but as your life is now exactly where it should be, within the spiral of time, the negative balance on the scales is moving much more strongly toward the positive."

Deacon gazed into his father's face. When he finally managed to speak, Deacon's voice betrayed his mixed feelings about what he had just heard. "So that unknown spaceship I saw through my binoculars when I was ten, was real!" A sense of relief flooded over Deacon as he recalled that eventful night many years before, the memory always having been an uncomfortable one.

"Yes, son." The reply was reassuring. "Once the coming storm is over, neither you nor Jett will remember how you actually made it through. And you won't even be sure when the storm has finally passed. You need to know that there will be a sequence of events which will provide you with information to carry out your quest. The part you and Jett will play is vital in ensuring the survival of the Crystals."

His father continued, "In time, I'm sure you will make an excellent leader like your grandfather, Colonel Rainer. I am eternally grateful to him for fulfilling the responsibilities of a father for you. He also has a significant part to play in the unfolding of your future."

The wind picked up again and the strange whispering sounds became louder. Deacon took his eyes off his father, moving his position slightly to get a better look up into the sky. His eyes grew wide as an intense ray of golden light streamed down through the white clouds.

In awe, he watched as a strange radiance slowly enveloped his father's body. There was a moment when their eyes met. His father nodded his head and gave a salute, and then he vanished. Deacon was alone on the porch.

"No, Dad! Don't go! I have so many questions!" Deacon pleaded and pleaded, tightly gripping the edge of the doorframe. For a moment, Deacon thought he could still hear his father speaking, although the words quickly faded as if someone was turning down the volume on a radio.

Finishing her preparations to treat her son's injuries, Lucy heard Deacon's muffled voice. She walked quickly down the hall, holding the first aid kit in one hand and ice cubes wrapped in a towel in the other. Looking ahead, Lucy saw a single flash of light at the front door.

"Deacon, what was that?"

Deacon, who was still standing in the doorway, took a deep breath and twisted round to look at his mother. He didn't want to think about the fact that he'd just lost his father for a second time. A baffled expression crossed his face as he struggled to comprehend the full meaning of his father's words. "D-D-Dad!" he stuttered.

A warm smile lit up Lucy's thin face. She studied her son intently, checking his dark eyes. "I think you may have concussion, son. Come and sit down again.

"I don't know who you thought you were talking with, but the reality is that your father's been dead for years. Your dad remains deep in our hearts and his memory lives on—a wonderful man taken from us far too soon. Memories of him often come flooding back to me during the night. Most of all, I see him in you.

"Now, come and sit on the sofa again. Let me clean up this blood and put some ice on that bump of yours. You need to get some rest. Jett's coming over later this afternoon. He called a while ago, when you were outside."

Deacon let out a groan as she gently dabbed at the blood congealed on his forehead. He groaned again when she stuck a plaster firmly over the graze.

The more she looked at her son and the more she thought about his words, the more Lucy was convinced that Deacon might be telling the truth. She recalled several occasions when she believed she'd seen a vision of her late husband, but had dismissed these sightings as part of the grieving process.

Deacon stretched his long legs sideways over the

russet-colored sofa. There was a mysterious glint in his mother's blue eyes as she placed the ice pack carefully on his head. He watched her turn and walk back toward the kitchen. In the stillness, comforting sounds echoed throughout the house—the click of the kettle, followed by a rumble as it set itself to boil; the clatter of cups being put out on the sink; and the tinkle of spoons. Lucy wasn't discreet in her movements, and she didn't creep around silently.

Leaning back into the cushions again, he closed his eyes. The coolness of the ice began to soothe his aching head. As Deacon drifted off to sleep, his mind slipped into a dreamlike state, traveling back to the age of ten, when it all began.

# *2*

# *Time Shared*

Retired army colonel, Antonio Rainer, was sitting in his living room one evening with Governor, his eight-year-old golden retriever. This room was on the lower level of his two-story house in North Florida, on the same boulevard as his daughter-in-law Lucy and ten-year-old grandson Deacon. The old soldier sat quite still for some time, focusing on the silence. He was acutely aware of the room stretching away from him in all directions. Since losing his wife Leeza to cancer, his large house had become lonelier and lonelier. "Maybe I should call Deacon tomorrow," he mumbled to Governor. Finally, he stood and then hauled himself up the stairs to his bedroom. He fell into bed with a groan.

The next morning, Colonel Rainer woke with a start. His dark eyes opened wide as he heard the sounds of voices and creaking floorboards downstairs. Soon realizing it was only Deacon and Lucy, the colonel ran his fingers through his short white hair, annoyed at being woken up. There was nothing more frustrating to him than his grandson's futile efforts to be quiet. Dragging himself out of bed, he quickly showered and dressed.

As he paused at the top of the stairs, with arms folded across his broad chest, the colonel realized that the house was now a hive of activity. He began to descend, and then stopped to cast an eye over the living room. Lucy had opened every curtain to the full. With all that light pouring in and the aroma of freshly brewed coffee and pancakes filling the morning air, it didn't feel like his house at all. Instead, it reminded him of his late son's house years ago, warm and welcoming.

For a few moments, he stood still and silently observed his grandson. The boy was sitting in a patch of sunlight, doing a new jigsaw puzzle, with Governor sitting on most of the pieces. Governor's tail began to flick excitedly from side to side, causing Deacon to glance upward.

With a broad smile on his face, Deacon said, "Morning, Grandpa. Mom's in the kitchen making ricotta pancakes for breakfast. Hope you're hungry?"

As their eyes met, Grandpa couldn't help but notice the look of admiration in his grandson's eyes. "Of course I am," he answered, struggling to keep the gruff tone out of his voice.

Governor stood up and ambled over to greet his master. After he received a quick rub around the ears, he headed off toward his bed, eyeing a chewy bone.

"Breakfast is served, Grandpa," Lucy said cheerily.

Colonel Rainer sank into his chair as she placed a full plate in front of him. He ate in silence, enjoying each mouthful. Afterward, he flashed a bright smile of thanks to Lucy. The two of them chatted for a while, allowing Deacon to finish his puzzle.

When it was time for Lucy and Deacon to leave, Grandpa and Governor walked out onto the front porch and waved good-bye. They kept watch till Lucy's shiny new car disappeared from view. "C'mon, fella. Let's go inside," the Colonel said wistfully and closed the front door. On his way down the long hallway to the living room, he muttered something under his breath.

The colonel made himself comfortable in his favorite chair and tried to relax. His eyes rested on a well-worn, multihued blanket; more memories came flooding back. Mrs. Mabbs, a kind neighbor of Lucy's, had crocheted it for him many winters ago after Leeza passed away. Finally, he could bear the silence no longer. He made himself a strong coffee and took it out onto the back porch. As he sipped his coffee, he watched Governor rolling around on the soft lawn and basking in the sun.

It was a humid, motionless day. Rainer sat himself down on a comfy deck chair and spoke to Governor, almost expecting the dog to answer back. Staring blankly at his feet, he became deep in thought. "Retirement has given me so much time, and ample opportunities to spend it with Deacon. But where do I start?"

With a flash of inspiration, he seized the moment. Grabbing his cell phone, he called Deacon. He was pleasantly surprised to discover they were both interested in the mysteries of the planets, and were equally familiar with the recent discoveries being made on Mars. It wasn't long before they were laughing together. Deacon's laugh was a carefree sound, full of life; Grandpa realized that this was a sound he had been longing to hear.

After a few trips, they became regular Saturday night visitors at an astronomical observatory some forty miles away on Samson Hill. One summer evening, at nine o'clock, Grandpa, Deacon, and Governor strolled through the parking lot. As they climbed the steep stone steps, Grandpa asked Deacon what was on the evening's agenda.

"Aliens!" Deacon exclaimed.

Grandpa chuckled, remembering his own fascination at a similar age with creatures from outer space. The trio proceeded to walk through the crowded parklands toward the lookout.

The air was pleasantly warm. Five minutes later, they arrived at their usual observation site, some distance from the crowd. Grandpa unrolled a blue-and-green checkered picnic blanket and spread it out on the grass. In the center he placed a generous picnic hamper that Lucy had provided for their supper.

Deacon unpacked his binoculars and then helped Grandpa connect their telescope to its tripod, placing a sturdy wooden crate beneath the instrument. The boy stepped onto the box and focused the lens. The evening seemed promising with not too many clouds.

"Found any extraterrestrials yet, son?" asked Grandpa cheekily.

"No, but I've found Omega Centauri."

"Wow! Let me take a look." After a few minutes Grandpa added, "I can see it too! It's like a globe-shaped stellar city, swarming with millions of stars. Do you know how many stargazers have this particular cluster on their bucket list?"

"No, but I can now cross it off mine." Deacon giggled.

They continued with their conversation for several minutes, discussing comets, shooting stars, and various constellations. Then Deacon lowered the telescope, skimming over the pine forest below. The needle-like foliage swayed back and forth, moaning softly in the strong breeze. He climbed off the box, sat on the blanket, and grabbed a cupcake. Noticing Governor sitting on his binoculars, Deacon jumped to his feet again. He leaned down, giving Governor a rub around the ears as he retrieved the binoculars from beneath the hairy body.

"Whose idea was it to send me these binoculars for my birthday, Grandpa? Was it yours or Mr. Allard's?"

"Why?" Grandpa asked.

"Well, Jett and I were talking about them yesterday. We don't think they look like normal binoculars. They seem far too advanced and complicated to be found in any store around here. So we searched the Internet and couldn't find them there either. By the way, what does Mr. Allard do in his spare time now he's retired?" Deacon took a bite of his mother's delicious cupcake.

The colonel didn't respond straight away. Instead, he reached for his water bottle.

"Are you listening to me, Grandpa? What does Mr. Allard do in his spare time now that he's retired?" repeated Deacon, swinging around to face him.

Grandpa sat still and studied Deacon's face before answering. "Colonel Allard heard about an elite telecommunications company dealing solely with undisclosed agencies inside the government sector. The business is located in France, in a city called Marseille. It's a very old port city on the Mediterranean Coast. Allard became interested in the company after a close associate of his confirmed that it was up for sale. The colonel immediately approached the proprietor, made a substantial offer, and bought it."

"Is that why he sends me neat gadgets from his secret

lair, all the way from France? Maybe Mr. Allard put some kind of bionic eye into the binoculars' lenses. Maybe it's secretly downloading and transmitting images I capture. I know there's something special about these binoculars. When I start to focus, I hear clicking sounds, and then everything becomes super clear."

Grandpa pursed his lips and frowned. "Wow, what an imagination! Yes, I was aware he wanted to send you something inventive from his new business. Maybe there is something extra special about those binoculars that I'm not even aware of, but I don't think Mr. Allard would be too impressed if he heard you calling his company a 'secret lair.'"

Deacon laughed, rolling onto his back and closing his eyes for a few moments. He thought about his extraordinary binoculars and imagined Mr. Allard planting some kind of gadget inside them. He also wondered what could possibly lie within the walls of Mr. Allard's top-secret hideout.

As the soft moonlight bathed his face, he opened one eye. Then he sat bolt upright with both eyes wide open. "Wow! Was that a meteorite?" Deacon began crawling around on his hands and knees, frantically rummaging around for his binoculars.

# 3

## *Deacon's Sighting*

"Did you see that? Maybe it was a UFO!" Deacon exclaimed.

"Yes, son, I did. So-called falling stars look quite extraordinary," replied Grandpa, ignoring Deacon's last comment. He grinned and raised his head, peering into the starry sky.

After reclaiming his binoculars, Deacon sat with his legs stretched out in front of him and continued to search for mysterious objects. Another expedition was becoming loaded with a whirlwind of fun and surprises.

Without warning, a sharp cracking sound echoed throughout the precinct.

"Look, Grandpa!"

A carnival was in full swing just beyond Samson Hill. Massive columns of vibrant hues and magnificent starbursts tore across the darkening sky. Sparkling cherry-red hearts scattered in every direction. The enormous explosion caused many of the stargazers to rush toward platforms on the edge of the hill, where they could marvel at the spectacular fireworks unfolding before them.

Deacon held his grandfather's hand tight, enthralled by the profusion of color. A grin appeared on Grandpa's face at the thought of another precious memory being made. This incredible event was a real crowd pleaser. When the majestic show reached its dazzling finale and faded into darkness, the hundreds of onlookers slowly dispersed.

Governor, however, had not appreciated the fireworks. "Could I please take Governor for a walk, Grandpa? I think he's restless. I won't be long," asked Deacon.

"Sure, go ahead, son," replied Grandpa. Deacon grabbed hold of Governor's leash. But Deacon hadn't gone very far when he heard the sound of a familiar but hostile voice. It made his blood run cold. Behind him came the swift shuffle of several booted feet along the concrete pavement.

Deacon tried to force a look of cool apathy to hide the hot tightness of his face. Bravely, he turned around. He mumbled, "Damn it!" when he saw his mean adversary from school, Karp Clydov, approaching out of the shadows with his gang. Taking a few deep breaths, he stared at Karp, desperately holding himself together. With his right hand, Deacon tightened his grip on Governor's leash, while holding his left hand rigid by his side. This was the only outward indicator that Deacon was anything but calm and collected.

"Well, look who's here, guys! Deek the freak! Is the doggy taking you for a walk, Deeky boy?" Karp sneered with a menacing, toothy grin.

Karp was almost a head shorter than his classmates, and so skinny that he looked lighter than a feather duster; his hands had long, spindly fingers. He was a smart kid who didn't do any homework and yet still got full marks. Having parents who didn't believe in setting boundaries, Karp had become a menace. He was very good at computer games, but preferred hacking the e-mail accounts of other students.

Deacon and Karp were rivals for top of the class in science. Out of spite, Karp had recently destroyed a pet project of Deacon's, a greenhouse ecosystem. Karp's uncle, Professor Clydov, doted on his nephew and was eager to have Karp join him at Clydovix International, a scientific research facility, after the completion of his schooling.

Karp's gang was a peculiar-looking bunch. One boy had an unusually long nose and a shaved head; he was dressed in a long green T-shirt and baggy pants. Another two were taller, with white paint smeared on their faces, making them look like ghouls. Following behind was an older boy with long, straggly brown hair that dangled way past his skinny neck. "Hey freak! Make Karp angry, so we can watch him smash your pretty face!" shouted one of the tyrants, stopping only a few feet away from where Deacon stood.

"What are you doing here, maggot?" Karp's voice was menacing as he edged closer.

"I could ask you the same thing," Deacon snapped, bravely facing up to his enemy. Governor sensed Karp's hostility. With a low growl, he wove his way protectively in front of Deacon. Karp ignored the dog and lunged aggressively at Deacon's ribs with a boney elbow. Deacon jumped clear and glared at Karp. The bully just laughed. He liked to mock people to make them angry.

Deacon bit his lip. He was so upset that he almost burst into tears, but he had learned a long time ago never to show Karp any form of emotion. Struggling to control trembling hands, Deacon stood his ground, wondering what to do next as the gang continued to taunt him. Governor barked.

Responding to his dog's signal, Grandpa excused himself from a conversation he was having with a friendly bystander and looked over in Deacon's direction. In less than a minute, he was at Deacon's side, towering over the group. Without saying a word, Grandpa raised an eyebrow and indicated to his grandson to move out. As he departed with Governor, Deacon returned Karp's dark stare.

Deacon's nervous tension began to ease as they left Karp and his cronies behind.

"Think we'll call it a night, Deek. It's getting late," Grandpa suggested.

"Fine with me," the boy muttered, as he slouched along beside his grandfather, anger surging inside of him.

"What's on your mind, Deek? D'you wanna talk about it?"

"I hate those boys! End of discussion!" he shouted. Deacon expected his grandfather to say something, but the man took a deep breath first.

Grandpa opened his mouth ready to pour scorn on the bully but then changed his mind. "Son, let me tell you a story that I used to tell your father. He often felt the same way you do about kids like Karp and his followers. They are children who take no responsibility for their actions. The hatred inside them will drag you down while it may not seem to affect them whatsoever. If it's any help to you, I've struggled with similar feelings of animosity many times during my life. Sometimes you feel as though there are two wolves living inside your body. One wolf is kind and does no harm. He is happy just to exist and doesn't take offense at criticism. He only does battle when it's the right thing to do, and in the correct way. However, the other wolf is foolish. The smallest incident will send him into fits of rage.

He fights with everyone all the time, even without cause. Unable to use reason, he gives full rein to his emotions which are fueled by anger and hatred. But it's all a waste of time and energy. It will change nothing. I think everyone finds it hard to live with these two wolves at times. They compete with each other in their attempts to dominate our character."

Deacon peered into his grandfather's dark brown eyes. "So tell me, Grandpa, which wolf wins?"

"The one you choose to feed, my boy. Come and help me pack up our gear."

In silence, they dismantled the telescope. Deacon rolled up the picnic blanket and ran around picking up food scraps, filling a small bag. He spotted a trash can nearby and called Governor. Side by side, they hurried along the fence line toward it.

On their return, the trio moved toward the steps leading down to the parking lot. Deacon thanked his grandfather for his support. Grandpa smiled and ruffled his grandson's dark curls. Skillfully changing the subject, he gave Deacon some thrilling news from the research center. The *Marc II* spaceship, which had just arrived on Mars, had already started sending back some remarkable information. The center's annual exhibition date had been changed because they needed time to process the data. Advances in technology meant that this spacecraft, equipped with an encapsulated robotic probe, had the ability to take off again from Mars, returning the capsule to Earth at the completion of its mission.

"Could we invite Jett to come along next weekend?"

"Already organized with parents, and tickets have been purchased."

"You're the best, Grandpa! Thank you!"

Before Grandpa could reply, Deacon clambered quickly down the steps and raced around the parking lot, followed closely by Governor. They sat on the ground near the car and waited for Grandpa to catch up. He arrived a few minutes later and stood near the four-wheel drive, the proximity key in his pocket. Doors unlocked and the trunk popped up. As he loaded the equipment into the vehicle, his two passengers climbed in. Deacon buckled the dog's harness and whispered into Governor's ear, "I can't wait. Jett's coming over tomorrow."

As the car moved out onto the road, Deacon mentioned wistfully that he hadn't sighted a single alien. Grandpa chuckled, shaking his head. "Maybe the fireworks chased them away. I'm sure you boys will come across plenty of strange creatures at the fair."

"But they're not real," Deacon moaned from the backseat, fumbling around inside his knapsack till he found his binoculars. Through the open car window, he scanned the night sky, anywhere and everywhere. Suddenly, the secret bionic eye in the binoculars detected an unfamiliar object.

Deacon's eyes grew wide as he caught a glimpse of something horrendous tearing its way through the outer reaches of the solar system. The bionic eye activated. It captured hundreds of images and downloaded them onto an advanced computer chip. Transmission began. As Deacon focused the lenses, he heard a strange clicking sound, but chose to ignore it. Instead he concentrated on a flash, little more than a circular distortion. Gas and dust streamed in from the surrounding area, briefly enclosing an evil-looking spacecraft in a mantle of blinding light. Actinic radiation streamed from the dwindling dust cloud. The vessel now seemed to be stationary, suspended in the middle of a glowing dust cloud, close to a familiar planet. Deacon knew instinctively that Mercury was under attack!

Deacon let out an ear-splitting scream. His panic-stricken grandfather slammed on the brakes and pulled up on the edge of the mountain road. He twisted around and stared at his distraught, wide-eyed grandson. Governor had already sensed the change in Deacon's mood.

"What's wrong, son?"

Deacon's heart almost leaped out of his chest. "There's an alien spacecraft inside our solar system, Grandpa! It's attacking Mercury!" he shrieked in panic.

"Settle down, Deacon! You've been reading too many comics!"

"But my binoculars started to make that strange clicking noise again. There is definitely something weird inside these binoculars. Anyway, I saw this horrible spaceship! I did, Grandpa!"

Grandpa confiscated Deacon's binoculars and rumbled sternly, "No more talk of aliens now! We still have a long drive ahead of us."

"Fine," blurted Deacon, falling back into the seat and angrily crossing his arms.

# 4

## *Family Friends*

$\mathcal{B}$right and early the next morning, Colonel Rainer stood on his front porch and waited for Governor to retrieve the Sunday newspaper from the front lawn. He sneaked a look up the street toward Deacon's house. The cloud-soaked sun was still low in the sky, throwing the trees into relief on the sidewalk and making the dew sparkle on the grass. When Governor returned with the paper, Rainer clicked the front door shut. Together they walked through the big house, their steps echoing on the hard tiles of the entrance hall and the hand-scraped ash floors.

It appeared to be a typical Sunday morning as Rainer made himself comfortable in his deck chair on the back porch, a piping hot coffee set beside him. That is, until he opened the newspaper. The colonel stared wide-eyed at the front page.

The headline screamed, "Strange Sightings from Samson Hill." The lede was compelling: "A mysterious object was seen soaring in the skies over North Florida last night. A great tail trailed across the sky, and then there was a flash of light. Many wondered if it was a UFO or possibly a comet. However, it was neither. It was only a new type of missile being tested by the navy. There were no casualties."

Grandpa sighed. He wasn't looking forward to the inevitable confrontation with his grandson. He read the story twice through his thick-lensed glasses and mumbled, "Well, how about that!"

Deacon also woke early, not long after sunrise. He jumped out of bed, flew down the stairs, and ran outside to grab the morning paper. Opening it up, he gasped when he read the headline. Anger washed over him. He felt as though someone had hit him hard, causing his breath to catch in his chest.

Anger was replaced by confusion. The story reinforced what he knew he had seen, but the explanation didn't fit. *Surely there has to be someone who knows what really happened. Why would the newspaper release such a ridiculous article?* he thought. "It's all lies," he yelled loudly. Everything seemed so complicated and infuriating at the same time. Impulsively he ran inside, clutching the newspaper in one hand and reaching for the phone with the other. Then he let the paper fall to the ground.

"Good morning, Grandpa! Have you seen the newspaper yet?" Deacon said, sounding annoyed and shaking his fist at the paper. "Can you believe it?"

"Yes. Just read it, son." Rainer raised an eyebrow, but his voice remained calm.

Deacon continued, "What were they thinking? A navy missile? I know what I saw last night and it was not a missile! Grandpa, do you believe me?"

"For what it's worth, I believe you."

"Thanks. That's all I needed to hear. Jett's coming over soon. I need to go now. We'll talk later. Good-bye!"

Grandpa became thoughtful as he hung up the phone. "Maybe I should keep an open mind for the sake of my friendship with Burnell Allard. I do have a vague memory of him saying something about those binoculars being rather special. Could it be that Deacon did capture images of a spaceship?" Grandpa picked up the paper again and spent an hour flicking through page after page, absentmindedly scanning minor news items, weather forecasts, and sports results.

He was startled by the ringing of his phone. "Bonjour, Tony! Burnell speaking."

A thought flashed through Rainer's head. *Is this a coincidence, Burnell calling from France today?*

After a brief chat about family matters, Burnell disclosed the real reason for his call. Tony, a little apprehensive at first, listened closely to his friend's explanation of what lay behind the fabricated headlines flashing around the world.

Tony responded, "I spoke with Deacon earlier today. He wasn't at all pleased to learn that his sighting was described as a new missile being tested."

"Listen carefully," Burnell said in a serious tone. "You cannot believe what you see or hear in the media, or even rely on what you think you already know. We're living in a time of terrible deception, and that deception is everywhere: it's in the media and in government. It's throughout society and permeates every civilization in the world. Turn on your computer, my friend. I'll send you what Deacon's binoculars actually captured!"

In minutes, the entire sequence downloaded. A long, flat prow, like the tip of a spear, was twisting in a kaleidoscopic display of pyrotechnics. Lightning flashed along the sides of a gigantic spaceship as it traveled through the solar system. The intruder was brutish and ugly, its exterior a drab, gunmetal gray, and its only decoration a brazen reptilian head. The eyes of an evil warlord could be seen glaring from inside the ship's prow. In the background, Omega Centauri, the largest globular star cluster in the Milky Way, was visible, glistening against the darkness. With a flash of blinding light, the craft penetrated straight through Mercury's energy field.

Rainer couldn't believe it.

The men's excitement was almost childlike as they discussed the horrific imagery that dominated their screens. About an hour and a half later, they said their good-byes.

Meanwhile, back at Deacon's house, the boy was still feeling confused and disappointed. At least, he was glad Jett was coming over soon. He decided to go outside and wait for his friend to arrive. From the front porch, Deacon spotted Mrs. Mabbs, his eccentric next-door neighbor. She was bending over a border of cheerful red and orange flowers beside her cobblestone path. As he approached the side fence, Deacon overheard her exclaim to a brightly colored garden gnome, "Oh, how I love the rich colors of summer flowers! Don't you?" Deacon's mood began to lift and he laughed softly to himself.

Mrs. Mabbs found the summer heat oppressive at times but she was not one to complain. Other neighbors were always grumbling about the weather and often gossiped among themselves about her as well. The old lady just ignored them. She was content with her short, squat body shape. Her long, iron-gray hair, tied loosely in a bun, was often greasy. Mrs. Mabbs wasn't concerned about the cataracts that were beginning to cloud her deep-set hazel eyes; they still twinkled when she smiled. She didn't worry either that her smile revealed several unsightly gaps in her yellowing teeth. Mrs. Mabbs's idea of aging gracefully was to let nature take its course.

Deacon wasn't interested in what other people thought of his unconventional neighbor. He valued Mrs. Mabbs's friendship and found her company interesting. He enjoyed visiting her in her unusual house, with its abundance of weird, homemade trinkets. Mooch, an old black cat with white feet, shared her home, keeping her company. Deacon sometimes saw Mrs. Mabbs toddling around in her garden, mumbling to Mooch. He was amazed how Mrs. Mabbs often knew what he was going to say before he said it, and wondered at her insightfulness.

After she finished chatting with the gnome, Mrs. Mabbs stood up. Her wooden Japanese sandals click-clacked along the path. She stopped and turned around when she heard Deacon's voice. Mooch flattened one ear, as cats do, swiveling her head in his direction.

"Good morning, Mrs. Mabbs. How are you doing today?" Deacon called out across the fence.

"Well, hello there! I'm doing well, thank you," she answered jubilantly.

"I'm waiting for Jett to arrive," he announced as he reached the fence. His face lit up when Mooch jumped up onto the inner railing. Deacon felt an irresistible desire to give her a rub under the chin.

Just then, Jett's mother pulled up in her car. Deserting Mooch, Deacon made for the sidewalk. Jett kissed his mom good-bye, opened the door, and leaped out of the passenger seat, giving his friend a high five. Dr. Stoen leaned across the seat and said hello to Deacon.

"Good morning, Dr. Stoen. Off to work?"

"Yes, I'm afraid so. The trauma ward is always short-staffed. Have a great day, boys!"

"Sure will. Thanks, Mom."

"Good-bye, Dr. Stoen!"

The boys waved as Dr. Stoen drove off down the quiet suburban street and then spun around ready to go toward the house. Jett caught sight of Mrs. Mabbs and greeted her with a friendly wave.

"Hello, Jett," she called out with a smile.

"Good morning, Mrs. Mabbs."

The boys stood still when they saw that Mrs. Mabbs was making her way eagerly toward them. She brushed past a marjoram bush and caused it to release its delicate fragrance. Nestled in the pocket of her faded orange, tie-dyed dress was a rough piece of aquamarine, a crystal believed to have powers of revelation. As she touched it, she felt the energy flow through the blue-green gemstone, alerting her to Deacon's inner turmoil. She caressed it with her fingers and received a brief insight. *Hmm … This crystal might help me discover the hidden meaning behind Deacon's experience last night*, she thought. Threads of her pale indigo aura seeped from her fingertips, covering the stone.

A strange scent, similar to sage, wafted through the air. Catching a whiff of it, Jett took a step backward. This allowed Mrs. Mabbs to reach out and touch Deacon's arm gently. She stared into his dark eyes. For a moment, the old woman saw visions of recent, disturbing images. A dull gray spaceship came flashing into view. She caught her breath as she glimpsed the sporadic pictures temporarily coming to life, a twisted, kaleidoscopic display of pyrotechnics. She hadn't seen visions like this in a very long time.

At that moment, Lucy appeared on the porch to greet Jett. Deacon shouted excitedly, "Mom, can we visit with Mrs. Mabbs for a minute?"

"Sure, honey, just don't stay too long."

"Okay," he replied, although he knew from past experience that it wasn't always possible to keep track of time while in the company of this eccentric old lady.

"Come along, boys," Mrs. Mabbs said in a soft, enticing voice. Deacon scooped Mooch off the fence and carried her down the cobblestone path. Deacon and Jett giggled between themselves as they hurried to catch up to their host. It was bright outside now, and the sun felt hot on their faces. As he approached the front door, Jett peered into the living room. There were several old sofas and chairs, and suspended on one wall was a television with a cartoon showing. Several brightly colored, half-finished crocheted blankets hung in a tangled mess on the back of an old rocking chair.

Mrs. Mabbs held the door open while Deacon and Mooch slipped through first, followed closely by Jett. Deacon glanced up at some yellow lights scattered on the high ceiling near the foot of the staircase. These weren't actually producing much light, but they added to the unusual atmosphere of the house.

Deacon put Mooch down as they followed Mrs. Mabbs into her small kitchen at the back of the house. They watched with anticipation as she took a bottle of milk and a plastic container out of the fridge. She proceeded to remove a delicious-looking chocolate cake from the container, cutting three huge slices and pouring three glasses of milk.

There was much scraping of kitchen chairs as everyone eagerly sat down. Mrs. Mabbs turned toward Deacon, hoping that he would be keen to talk about the visions she had seen when she touched his arm. Her curiosity was hard to contain.

"Now, Deacon," she coaxed, after they'd had a minute or two for a few bites of cake. "Tell me about what you saw last night." She leaned forward and peered closely at him over the top of her glasses.

Deacon, rather shocked, returned her stare.

She hardly dared to breathe. Would he reveal everything to her?

To give himself time to recover, the stunned boy took another bite of cake. *How come she knows about that?* he wondered.

Mrs. Mabbs believed he was hiding something big. The meaning of what he'd seen probably remained a mystery to him—one he was completely oblivious to at such a young age. But she sensed that he had a very clear memory of what he had witnessed.

Concentrating hard, Mrs. Mabbs examined the outline of Deacon's aura. A fresh breeze caused the trees to beat on the glass like impatient fingers. As she stared out at her garden stretching away from her, the reason for her unusual mood slowly dawned on her. Strange visions kept coming into her mind, connected to the newspaper article she had read earlier this morning.

The old lady looked deeply into Deacon's eyes once more, and the muscles in the boy's jaw tightened. His mind was replaying the vivid memory of his sighting. She was surprised that Deacon's concentration didn't seem to be affected by Jett's obvious excitement. Instead, Deacon had a sense of calmness about him as he recounted the events of the previous night.

Jett and Mrs. Mabbs listened in silence. Mrs. Mabbs

became quite concerned when he described the evil-looking spacecraft. She was worried that the memory of it hovering above Mercury might cause him to wake in the night with his heart pounding.

Finally, the old lady smiled. Her hair hung down like rats' tails as she stared thoughtfully into Deacon's wide eyes. "This could be the beginning of something incredibly big. Everything that comes your way from now on should be seen as an opportunity. Don't worry if some people laugh at your extraordinary sighting. In the future, it will contribute to your strength. Although Jett and I believe you, others simply won't. If you're to fulfill your destiny and find great happiness, you must take note of everything and embrace every possibility. Perhaps there's a pattern to it all. Oh my, is that the time?"

"Thanks, Mrs. Mabbs, I think," Deacon said, looking a little puzzled.

Mrs. Mabbs waited for Deacon and Jett to finish their milk and cake. She wrapped a rosy pink, cotton shawl around her shoulders and cleared the table. Kissing each boy on the cheek, she sent them back next door.

Breathless and sweaty, Mrs. Mabbs rubbed her hands together. She paused for a moment, losing track of time and feeling dizzy with excitement in anticipation of the next vision. With a slight skip in her step, she bent down and picked up Mooch. Stopping in front of an antique mirror hanging in the hall, she stood still for a moment, looking at her reflection. An elderly woman stared back with a face that was all angles—deep wrinkles, sharp cheekbones, small chin, and thin nose. Mrs. Mabbs sighed and carried the cat into the living room.

Seated comfortably on the sofa with Mooch beside her,

Mrs. Mabbs took a deep breath and held it. She finally breathed out, whispering, "Oh, Moochie! Disaster has hit Mercury! The solar system is about to change forever. Deacon's sighting is true in its essence, if not complete in all details." She closed her eyes and began chanting to an imaginary tribal drum.

# 5

## *Hadesians*

"What do you think you're doing, knucklehead? You've just used ultra-warp drive to take us right into the middle of Omega Centauri! Do you want to get us vaporized?"

The navigator, Lieutenant Commander Razil, ignored his superior officer; he was mesmerized by the three hundred and sixty degree view surrounding him. He felt like a super sleuth ascending into greatness as the spacecraft twisted and turned through the massive globular star cluster. "Extraordinary!" he screeched.

"Maybe," yelled Girmlot, the commander, "but only a stupid idiot would dive headlong into a swarming hive of ten million stars!"

"Only a stupid coward would waste time taking the long way round! We made it through alive, didn't we? So stop your bellyaching!"

"Shut up, imbeciles!" bellowed the ship's captain, Obsidian, interrupting the volatile argument on the bridge of the *Zonosor*, his mammoth, Gothic-style vessel. The reptilian warlord's forked tongue flicked feverishly behind serrated teeth, while thick globs of saliva fell to the floor. His tail thrashed from side to side. This powerful, grotesque mockery of a human stood seven feet tall and was covered in scales; he appeared to his victims as a vision of malice.

Obsidian and his warriors came from a violent world known as Hades, an enormous planet in a parallel dimension. Hades was protected by a shield of infernos no normal spacecraft could penetrate and survive. The inhabitants, known as Hadesians, were a race of violent reptilian soldiers. Trained from their youth, these ferocious flesh-eaters were so fast and strong they could single-handedly defeat more than a dozen adversaries simultaneously, dispatching them effortlessly into the realm of the dead. The most powerful and successful warriors became warlords; Obsidian was the most ruthless one the planet had ever produced.

His mission was to travel across the cosmos from one universe to another, to seek out other worlds, especially peaceful civilizations, where the sacred writings of the gods were valued. The warlord took great pleasure in conquering each vulnerable planet, engaging in slaughter of epic proportions with his huge army of aggressive Hadesians.

Obsidian also plundered the planets he invaded. His warriors stole jewels, gases, and rare minerals, building up huge stockpiles of crucial supplies for the warlord's wicked empire. Huge cages, jam-packed with an assortment of animals, were hauled aboard the *Zonosor* for food.

With violence and terror, their devastation spread quickly. If Obsidian did decide to leave some inhabitants alive, hostile administrators were sent to rule over them. These would swiftly crush any resistance by the survivors.

The *Zonosor*, equipped with highly advanced technology

and weaponry, had now entered the Milky Way galaxy. As it emerged from Omega Centauri, the greedy warlord became exhilarated by the promising planetary system that appeared on the screen and ordered the lieutenant commander to set a course for the planet nearest the system's sun.

Obsidian's ruthless army easily conquered Mercury. No mercy was shown to the hapless inhabitants; all living creatures were either captured for food or cruelly annihilated. Resources were drained to provide fuel for the *Zonosor*.

Now ready to move on, the captain stood on the bridge of his spacecraft, raised a long, claw-shaped finger, and scratched his scaly face like a cat. "Show me what I can find on the next planet," he demanded. The commander hurriedly brought up information about Venus on the electromagnetic screen.

Focusing his lustful eyes on this data, Obsidian's thin lips broadened into a cruel smile. In an arrogant tone he sneered, "What do we have here now? The planet of love and beauty, eh? My next target, I believe! I'll enjoy destroying it. Love is illogical and inefficient. Beauty is senseless, a waste of time! I will continue in my quest to conquer every planet I can find, until my fellow flesh-eaters and I have erased all weak life-forms. Then I will bring the cosmos under my control. I will eliminate all love."

As Obsidian zoomed in on the screen, the laser pulses gave him more information about Venus. While it did seem to be enclosed in some kind of protective force field, he could see it would prove useless against the *Zonosor*. He was also able to ascertain that the native inhabitants, known as Crystallites, posed no threat to him or his legions, although there were some indications that the creatures might possess unusual technical abilities.

Highlighted areas of Venus showed many dark zones within luminous clouds; an incredibly vast network of tiny bright lights was also visible. As the warlord examined the tangled chains of burgundy, indigo, and yellow, the prospect of retrieving hydrogen, helium, and other ionized gases thrilled him immensely.

Breaking his concentration, Obsidian turned and hissed into the commander's grotesque face. Undeterred, his subordinate pointed at the screen with a long, gnarled finger, growling in a guttural voice, "Take a look at the available assets just waiting for us! Valuable jewels, exotic animals and fruit, an abundance of minerals, and mineshafts loaded with gold. It's unbelievable! It will all be ours!"

*What a treasure trove!* thought the greedy warlord. He flicked his forked tongue as thick drool dripped from his half-opened mouth in anticipation.

Brighter areas of color showed there were also massive amounts of electromagnetic radiation. As the captain watched the waves on the screen, he noticed that they became more intense as they moved from one end of the spectrum to the other. Somehow the planet's energy existed as both protons and waves at exactly the same time. This was indeed an extraordinary mystery! However, it was only the beginning of his discovery of the treasures the planet kept secreted away.

One of the most intriguing aspects of his target was a feature of the Crystallites themselves. They seemed able to produce their own unique form of natural power. Obsidian bellowed out an explicit order—the capture and imprisonment of twenty-five Crystallites.

He flicked his display sideways, and the name "Elderflower Elixir" appeared on the screen. Obsidian read with interest about small insects known as bees, which produced a strange, gooey, gold substance known as honey. Along with certain exotic fruits, honey was a key ingredient in the secret recipe for this elixir. An incredibly powerful potion, it was rumored to transform ordinary mortals into immortal gods. Learning this, the warlord became frenzied with anticipation, flicking his forked tongue, drooling, and hissing.

"This planet is priceless! I'll find this elderflower drink and become a god! Immortality is within my reach! I'll make barrels of the stuff. I'll drink it all!" he boasted.

The captain stomped across the room, his tail thrashing violently from side to side. Girmlot had trouble keeping out of his way. Raising short, crooked arms, the warlord proceeded to dictate more orders. His minion left the bridge without delay. This planet was becoming more astounding by the minute. Obsidian fantasized about the extraordinary, unknown capabilities of the Crystallites.

# 6

## *Venus under Attack*

ematite stood on the top of the clock tower, looking thoughtful. With the fingers of one hand, he lightly traced the top of the railing, then paused. A cold chill raced down his spine as the elder caught sight of a huge, gray, metallic object descending from the clouds. Its shape was basically rectangular but curved. The ominous-looking craft broadening above him was surrounded by churning dust and gas, and appeared to be many times larger than his whole town. He craned his neck, cleared his throat, and swallowed as volatile bursts of light began to flash before his eyes. There was no way of telling what it was or why it was there, but he sensed danger.

The Crystallites of Venus were a mysterious, reserved community. With eyes of cerulean blue and flawless skin the color of pale bronze, they stood about four feet tall and were dressed in dazzling white garments, tied at the waist with golden cords. Delicate circlets, woven with rose scented flower buds, adorned their heads of ice-white curls that tumbled past thin shoulders. Exceptionally beautiful, their refined movements were comparable to the graceful, dance-like steps of a ballerina. They were full of love for each other and for Aphrodite, the goddess of love and beauty, who ruled their planet.

With mounting apprehension, Hematite continued to keep watch. He saw needle thin, impossibly long, indigo veins of light appear. Then the threads of an indescribable web of light merged together. Extended curves and strange circles created an uncontrolled framework inside a purple haze. Following the indigo flickers with his eyes, the elder noticed that the shafts of light were curling in unusual ways, giving the impression of four dimensions. The most disturbing part of all this was what it was doing to his mind. It felt as though his thoughts were spiraling into the spatial irregularities he was observing. The vision resembled an abstract work of art, painted in countless hues of ornate blues and purples; the effect on him was spine-chilling but inexpressibly beautiful at the same time. *Who or what is producing this eerie light show?* he wondered. In the whole of his one hundred and fifty years, he had never seen anything like this.

Several curious Crystallites stood in the town square and stared at the unusual light show overhead. Although it was magnificent and mysterious, it made them feel rather anxious, especially the dark gray shape lurking inside a thick dust cloud.

Onyx and Jade, aged five, were kicking a bright red ball around in Onyx's front garden. Onyx was keeping a lookout for bees when something else caught his attention. Strange purple lights shot out and flickered wildly, dancing above their heads. Onyx stepped up onto a rock to improve his view. There was an unfamiliar scent gusting from the north and the smell of exploding dynamite. He flashed a worried glance at Jade. Both spun round and dashed toward his front door.

Families scurried from every direction and streamed into the square. The inhabitants of Venus were used to their planet's normal disruptive motions. They knew that the ground beneath them could shift at any moment due to unstable plates far below. The surface of gigantic lakes sometimes swirled like water in a bathtub. Crystallites were well practiced at climbing into treetops and knew to be on the lookout for flying debris. But now they realized with increasing dismay that they were not at all prepared for this unexpected and possibly catastrophic situation.

The sunlight was fading; an apprehensive darkness began lurking everywhere. Many heard whispers of fearful happenings from older members of the community and were curious to know more. Aphrodite was the only one they could call on in times of great crisis. Without wasting any more time, Hematite sounded his bone-white conical horn, then hurried down from the clock tower to join those already in the square.

As the sound of the horn faded, the Crystallites were still wondering what the light show was all about. By this time, almost every man, woman, and child in the town had left their homes. Most of them had gathered in the square. They gazed northward toward the nearby mountains as they waited anxiously for their beloved goddess to respond.

Great columns of fiery gold flames appeared, silhouetting the majestic peaks that towered toward pink-tinged clouds. Soon they heard the turbulent flap of wings. There was something magical in the noise, something melodious. The glowing form of Aphrodite came into view in a golden, jewel-encrusted chariot drawn by five large white turtledoves. They cleared the mountaintops and soared over scattered villages and acres of flourishing gardens.

Aphrodite's appearance was breathtaking. Her long golden curls tumbled down beyond her sandals of woven flowers; her silken robe flashed, shimmering with vibrant reds and oranges. The goddess's skin was soft and milky white, radiating a heavenly glow. Her eyes were the same cerulean blue as those of the Crystallites, but more brilliant. She was adorned in jewelery of the finest gold and wore an elegant headdress made with fragrant pink crystal flowers.

Aphrodite pulled on the golden reins as she steered the chariot downward. Alighting on the ground in the middle of the town square, she beckoned her much-loved subjects nearer.

"Quick! There's not much time! Our planet is under attack! I have placed a silver force field around it to try to prevent an invasion, but I'm not sure how long my protection will hold up against this evil intruder. Take as many animals as you can carry and seek refuge among my forests and mountains."

A white turtledove flew overhead and pronounced, "Great harm awaits you! Now go!"

The elder waved to indicate a path heading straight for the nearest trees. The Crystallites quickly gathered up as many animals as they could carry and headed off. Those in the lead set a frantic pace.

In the crowded square, Onyx began to panic. He couldn't find his parents, Peridot and Topaz, and he'd also lost sight of Jade. In a desperate bid to find his friend, he rushed down a narrow cobblestone path that meandered through the trees, but she was nowhere to be seen. As he struggled to control his increasing fear, Onyx continued on through the forest alone.

Many enchanting sights came into view. He followed some animal tracks until they vanished among tangled vines and prickly shrubs. Onyx made his way through dense pine copses, clearings, and small pastures flooded with soft light from hundreds of pink crystal flowers. These special flowers of Aphrodite's glowed during the long days on Venus and then shone more brightly during the long nights that followed.

Onyx ran through rippling streams of crystal-clear water. The forest stretched on and on, and the ground became steeper and steeper. Out of breath, he finally decided to lie down and take a rest on the top of a ridge. He still hoped Jade might find him before it was too late, but there was no sign of her.

Once he had recovered, the boy decided to climb one of the tall trees nearby and take refuge among its thick green foliage. As he climbed his chosen tree, inquisitive forest animals leaping from branch to branch greeted him with their anxious chatter.

Through telepathy, he heard his father's concerned voice: *"Where are you, son?"* Poor Onyx couldn't keep the conversation going for very long. His eyes began to close. Within minutes he was fast asleep.

Meanwhile, Aphrodite sat nervously inside her chariot, flying slowly round and round, high above the ground. Panic gripped her when she realized the immense force field she had created around her beloved Venus was proving useless against the technology of the invading spacecraft. The *Zonosor* burst through the shield and hovered just above the surface of the defenseless planet.

The frightened goddess watched helplessly as scores of well-armed, ugly Hadesian warriors swarmed out and slid down a metal ramp that appeared from the ship's underbelly. They moved noiselessly toward their assigned areas. Waving fire torches and breathing heavily, one division surrounded the first tiny village. In a matter of minutes, the fragile houses were all burned to the ground. The bright glow from the torches flickered wildly, illuminating grotesque, scaly, reptilian faces. Any Crystallite caught trying to escape was instantly scorched like an insect and promptly devoured. Over and over again, this scenario was repeated with devastating results.

In the town, five panic-stricken families, including those of Onyx and Jade, had disobeyed Aphrodite and instead hurried to take refuge inside the library. They hid silently in the shadowy corners of the archives. When, through telepathy, Hematite realized what had happened, he rushed frantically back to find them before it was too late.

"Peridot, where's Onyx?" whispered the elder when he found them.

"He was separated from us in the confusion, but he's made it into the forest. I think he's asleep right now, high up in a tree on a mountain ridge. Hopefully he'll be safe," replied the concerned father, also in a whisper.

A piercing scream split the silence. Jade's voice was high and loud. Everyone looked up in horror, squinting in the light of a bright torch outside a window. Silhouetted by the torchlight, a massive, snakelike head rose up and glared through the tinted glass. Moments later, every window shattered into a thousand pink shards. Apple trees outside were instantly burned to a crisp. The library was under attack!

Doors burst open, tables were overturned, and books were flung from their shelves. The sound of heavy, rapid breathing came closer. *"Everybody! Quick! Come over here!"* Hematite sent the order by telepathy while waving his arm. Garnet grabbed her older daughters, Jade and Sunstone, by their hands. Bixbite gathered up their youngest daughter, Emerald, in his arms, as the evil warriors stormed through what was left of the building.

The fugitives raced from the ruins like a stampeding herd. Bixbite could hear the invaders' heavy breathing as he darted into the town square behind his friends, fearful of being eaten. He cried out, "I can't believe this is happening!"

One of the Hadesians glimpsed a snippet of white disappearing around a corner and gave chase, thick saliva dripping from his frightful jaws.

Hearing a crashing sound, Bixbite glanced backward. "Get down!" He grabbed Jade and Sunstone, pulling them to the ground. Everyone dropped onto their hands and knees at once and hid behind an enormous three-tiered water fountain.

The reptilian caught sight of Jade's flowery circlet and headed toward the fountain. He raised a huge, clenched fist and brought it down hard, smashing the whole structure. The sickening crack and the thud that followed were terrifying. Water rose high into the air, saturating everyone. A hole in the ground appeared where the fountain once stood.

The Crystallites made a frantic dash across the square, followed by heavy footsteps and torturous breathing. Waving his drenched, smoldering torch in the air, the irate warrior let out a terrible roar when he realized the fugitives were escaping.

Hematite was alarmed to find that the light from

the crystal flowers was beginning to fade; this had never happened before in the whole history of the planet. There was just enough light, though, for the elder to spot a tapering path leading toward the forest. He held up a finger and pointed to the partially lit lane. The Crystallites crawled on their hands and knees, trembling in fear. One behind the other, they crept along in silence.

As the forlorn band passed through the tree line, a brilliant flash lit up the foliage and blinded them momentarily. There was a deafening thump, and flames went soaring up into the clouds. Everybody felt the ground tremble. In an instant, the twenty-four of them were swooped up into an iron net. There wasn't a trace of emotion left on the tiny faces, only panic in cerulean blue eyes. Each one somehow knew that their captors were fighting off an urge to eat them instead of taking them prisoner.

# 7

## *Doomed*

The golden chariot dipped and rose on the air currents. Aphrodite was distraught. She had no idea where these bloodthirsty creatures came from or what they wanted. As her chariot circled, she searched in vain for a glimpse of white. Confronting Obsidian was now inevitable.

Aphrodite swallowed hard and her chest tightened as her chariot approached the *Zonosor*. The goddess strained her eyes. She could just make out a dark figure standing on a deck or platform, near the top of the spacecraft. Then another silhouette appeared and took up its position beside the first. Her chariot now hovered near the platform's thick metal railing.

Giant, gnarled, claw-shaped fingers lashed out at Aphrodite. With raised hands, she tried to protect her face. The goddess heard a sharp cracking sound as a vine lasso wrapped around the chariot. Abruptly, a dozen reptilian warriors appeared and heaved it closer. She screamed for help as blood gushed from a gouge on her left ankle. Digging her feet into the chariot's floor, she pulled hard on the golden reins, her teeth clenched and muscles strained. Aphrodite sensed that the reins were about to snap. Her five turtledoves struggled in desperation, trying to ascend. Her terrified eyes filled with tears, but she swallowed hard again, releasing the reins.

"Leave her alone! Fools! Go now! At once! She's all mine!" screamed Obsidian, now appearing beside the chariot. The reptilians disappeared into the background and left the goddess alone, trembling but alive, with their captain.

Aphrodite briefly closed her eyes and took a deep breath. Summoning all the courage she could, the frightened goddess stepped onto the platform and advanced warily toward her adversary, eyes blazing.

As her striking face rose up before him from the depths of the shadows, a strange feeling of ecstasy surged through the warlord's veins. The evil creature who despised beauty was mesmerized by the breathtaking vision before him. Her astonishing face with its piercing blue eyes was surrounded by lustrous golden curls. Not realizing what was happening to him, he gave her a dangerous smile. Thick, beige, nauseating phlegm slid past a burgundy tongue lashing beneath his bottom jaw. The warlord hissed through clenched teeth and tightened his grip on the railing.

Unable to contain her curiosity any longer, Aphrodite found her voice. "I demand to know who you are! Why have you come to make war against us? We have never harmed anyone!" A ripple of strong emotion passed over her face, leaving her blue eyes transfixed and soft lips partly open.

"I don't usually give my victims the pleasure of knowing anything about me before I devour them, but I'll make an exception in your case. You should be very grateful!"

Obsidian's voice was rough, but he still wasn't fully aware of his feelings and why he was behaving this way. "I am Obsidian, the most powerful warlord on Hades and possibly the whole universe!" he continued in a superior tone. "I have learned of the riches your rather primitive planet presents to me, so I am about to help myself. Now that my warriors are conquering your weak, sniveling creatures, I am claiming my right to drink the immortality potion, Elderberry Elixir, and take anything else I want. It's all mine! I will abolish all pitiful signs and symbols of love and beauty throughout the whole planet too!"

"Love? Why would you want to destroy love? Love doesn't destroy anyone. Instead, it sustains and strengthens all those who feel it. A true living being would trust that love always prevails, no matter what."

"Not on my watch! I am going to rule your precious planet from now on, and I will punish you for cultivating such a corrosive force!"

"How dare you insult us! What we stand for is truth!"

"I'm growing impatient, goddess. I hope you're finished with your futile resistance!" he sniggered, with a sly sense of playing a game.

Aphrodite was not amused. She returned to her chariot and sat down. Apart from her breathing, which was steady and controlled, the goddess remained motionless, as though she were invisible. Her long-lashed eyelids closed tightly. Obsidian began to suspect that her actions were a special performance for his benefit.

The warlord commented, "If you ask me, I think our goddess looks rather terrified." He leaned forward as Aphrodite opened her eyes. "Now, what could she possibly be afraid of? Why, it must be me! So tell me, goddess. Are you absolutely certain that love is stronger than hatred? Let there be a battle, then, between your love and my hate."

"Emotions cannot fight one another!" Aphrodite replied, agitated. "And why do you want to destroy the most peaceful planet within our system? We serve love. It is the one thing that will eventually bring peace and harmony to the rest of the universe. Haven't you ever felt love?"

"Yes, but I think its correct name is 'lust,'" he sneered.

The goddess ignored his reply. "I love everyone and everything within this entire galaxy."

Feeling like there was some kind of link developing between them, Obsidian continued, "Well now, goddess! That means you love me! We'll be married at once, and we'll drink your elderflower potion to celebrate. I too shall become immortal, and we'll be together forever!"

"Never! I would rather die!" Aphrodite shouted, somewhat surprised at the strength of her voice.

"So you don't love me after all? It sounds like you might even hate me! I declare that hatred has won the battle. It is stronger than love! If you don't agree with me, I'll slaughter the twenty-four of your precious Crystallites my warriors have just captured. They will make a fine feast. Yes, I'm beginning to feel rather hungry." His tone became more menacing; Aphrodite was startled by the change in his glassy black eyes. "Agree now to join me in matrimony or your planet will be annihilated!"

Aphrodite closed her eyes again, inhaled deeply, and raised her graceful arms. As her hands opened, rays of brilliant light streamed from her palms. A crystal ball of light was instantly created. It quickly soared upward with a comet-like tail forming behind. Silently it rocketed into the darkness of space. The fearful goddess prayed that her distress signal would be received somewhere before it was too late. Without help, she knew she faced an unbearable life trapped in Obsidian's oppressive world, condemned to an eternity of torment. But who could save her?

Before the warlord realized what was happening, Aphrodite flicked the reins firmly and the doves began ascending. They hauled their precious goddess away from the *Zonosor.*

As her chariot sailed up and up, her ears caught the sound of a huge, angry roar from Obsidian. "You come back here right now, goddess! At once! How dare you defy me! You'll be sorry!"

Quivering with amazement at her apparent escape, Aphrodite soared across the darkening heavens in her chariot and disappeared behind tall mountain peaks, desperately searching for a place where she might find sanctuary. The conflict would certainly escalate now. Using telepathy, the goddess began to speak to all her subjects throughout the planet, but in such a faint whimper that her words were barely audible. *"Get out of your homes at once. Hide anywhere you can. They are coming for you."*

Although the message was distorted, the remaining Crystallites understood that Obsidian had declared war.

***

On Mars, Ares was speaking with his father, Zeus, when a blazing, comet-like object entered the atmosphere. It exploded into shards of colored crystal light. "A distress signal from Venus!" exclaimed Ares. "Aphrodite must be in great peril to ask for help. Her force shield obviously wasn't effective against this invader!"

"Remember, Ares, that Aphrodite has helped your

planet in times past. Now you must return the favor. Hermes was too proud to ask for help when Mercury was under attack. His stubbornness caused that planet to suffer a most terrible fate. You must do whatever you can to save Venus."

Without further hesitation, Ares took the guise of a cloud and left Mars.

When he reached his destination, the god of war heard sounds of violent mantras echoing throughout the lands. He observed the *Zonosor* with its blood red flag.

Almost immediately, there began a series of enormous shudders as many grotesque Hadesians thundered across the lands. Some of the ferocious warriors tore blindly through the thickly wooded areas, snapping small shrubs and knocking down trees in their search for prey. Others took up positions amid the vegetation and behind huge rock formations to wait for fleeing Crystallites.

Sounds from distressed doves spread throughout the lands as countless fugitives crept away from their villages. Malevolent eyes followed one group as they traveled along a meandering lane which led into an orchard. Ambushed among the cherry trees, they had no escape. All were killed and eaten.

Some inhabitants from the town were making their way deeper into the forest. The youngsters staggered and stumbled along. Narrow paths were becoming difficult to see beneath their feet, as an increasing gloom erased them. The light from the crystal flowers was starting to grow dim, producing an eerie haze. Terrified Crystallites often glanced upward, desperately searching for a glimpse of Aphrodite's chariot.

A dozen fugitives made their way past a small blue lake. They scrambled quickly up a hillside, descended just as fast, and crossed a rippling steam. Behind them, a branch snapped. They could smell the vile stench of drool dripping constantly from frightful mouths.

"Look down! Over here! They're hiding among the ground cover!" roared a warrior.

"I see them! Their blue eyes are shining. Leave this lot to me!" another screeched.

Thick green grass rustled under the enemy's feet. Tiny persons looked fear in the eye and froze. Aggressive flames raged in front of them. Not a single life was spared.

Bloodcurdling screams continued to echo throughout Venus. Hordes of armed warriors slithered about, burning more and more villages and slaughtering more and more victims. Huge quantities of the enemy's lethal gases also caused the deaths of many of Aphrodite's innocent creatures. Most of the crystal flowers were dead, squelched into the ground.

Artillery units swept in, demolishing entire villages instantaneously. The invaders' widespread destruction was executed with ease. Automaton miners were unleashed and tore through mineshafts, stripping everything of value. Obsidian's obsessive desire for power was apparently insatiable. He was easily achieving yet another victory.

A loud crack ripped through one region. Onyx, high up in his leafy hideout on the ridge, woke with a start. Opening his eyes, he saw a warrior pitch forward, launch himself into the foliage, and land heavily nearby. The branches bent beneath the Hadesian's weight and brought Onyx down onto the forest floor. Leaves rained down, scattering on top of him. As he scrambled to his feet, Onyx tripped over some branches and lunged forward. He dodged left, right, and then left again, trying to escape. The brute threw a leg out into the small Crystallite's path. Onyx stumbled over his attacker's foot and rotated, landing right on the edge of the ridge. Slipping over it, he tumbled down in what felt like an endless fall. When he came to an abrupt halt, he was unable to move. Another reptilian caught sight of him, dredging him up triumphantly by the scruff of his neck. Onyx was captured: number twenty-five.

Scores of animals were being thrown into black metal cages. Agitated bees, trapped inside their hives, were shoved into dark storage containers. These, along with tubs of exotic fruits and heavy bags of gold, were lugged toward the *Zonosor*. On board, reptilians worked solidly, loading the booty onto a conveyor belt. It rumbled along to the hold, set deep within the vessel's underbelly.

From inside their metal cage, the frightened Crystallites heard shouts from deep, rough voices speaking with bad-tempered tongues: "Twenty-five celestial beings counted and caged."

When Onyx saw Jade's face squashed against thick steel bars, his heart sank. He tried desperately to think of a way to escape. Wanting reassurance and still sore after his tumble, the boy reached for his dad's hand but became distraught as his father whispered despondently, "I am so very sorry, my son. We are all trapped."

Obsidian, very pleased with the battle reports he was receiving, had retired to the captain's chambers, where he sat upon his ebony throne. But he wasn't feeling as satisfied as he usually did after a successful conquest. The unfinished business with Aphrodite angered him. "How dare she defy me, the mighty Obsidian!" he roared.

Just then Girmlot entered the room and announced, "One more miserable Crystallite has been added to the twenty-four already caught, Captain. You now have your twenty-five wretched creatures. I can't imagine what use they'll be to you except for a feast. But anyway, they're now caged."

The warlord grunted in reply and dismissed the commander with a wave of his stubby arm. Looking around, he caught sight of a crystal decanter sitting on an ebony table in the corner. It was filled with a shimmering bronze liquid. His beady eyes gleamed. Obsidian stood up and moved toward it, an evil grin spreading over his leathery face. "Amazing! My very own Elderflower Elixir! I shall reward the warrior who found it."

# 8

## *Crystal Lake*

A white turtledove soared across the gloomy sky. Urged on by the sound of its own breathing, the large bird flew over the devastated terrain of Venus with a message for Aphrodite. It headed low into a narrow valley where huge, reptilian warriors jumped up toward it, making wild grabbing gestures. Others tried chasing it from behind. "I only have a short time to deliver Ares's message," cried the dove as it realized the repulsive creatures had no intention of giving up. "If I can't fly faster, I'll be eaten for sure. If one of those horrible creatures grabs me, I'll never escape." The reptilian faces were daunting, and the bird kept a wary eye on them as it struggled to gain speed. Gaining height was not an option due to the overhanging crags.

With sheer determination and a watchful eye, the turtle dove made its way out of the valley. After maneuvering through a narrow gap between two rocky outcrops, the dove caught sight of Aphrodite's chariot, which now hovered above the summit of a nearby mountain. The goddess was surprised by the sound of turbulent wings growing louder.

As the bird spiraled higher and higher, it cleared the summit and then perched on the chariot's gold railing.

The dove caught its breath quickly, glanced around, and said in an urgent voice, "Ares was here for a short time, and he gave me a message for you. He said to send Obsidian to Mars. Tell the greedy warlord that Earth has just discovered a mysterious new form of electromagnetic power on Mars. The god of war has promised to try to protect your twenty-five captured children. He will come to you after he destroys Obsidian."

Although heartbroken by her traumatic ordeal, Aphrodite took some comfort from this message. She wasn't looking forward to returning to Obsidian but realized it was the only way to carry out Ares's instructions. Her stomach was in knots as she flicked the reins. The chariot glided effortlessly through thick clouds toward the *Zonosor* once more. Approaching the spacecraft, she heard the sounds of hissing and ignored the most dreadful insults that one could possibly imagine. A voice bellowed from the platform beneath her, causing her to tremble.

Aphrodite could only see a vague outline of a dark silhouette with massive shoulders. She felt rather than saw his beady black eyes watching her in veiled mockery. He tried to remain nonchalant, but his treacherous voice gave him away.

"The goddess of love and beauty! Here! Right before me! Are you ready to surrender to me now?"

Aphrodite's mouth went dry. Her hands shook and her lips quivered. "I have a proposition for you," she said, somehow finding the courage to speak.

"What is it? Speak up! I don't believe it will interest me though."

"You have come a long way through the spiral of time, searching for new ways to power your warship. Not many warlords can boast about that. How frustrating to wind up here, in this insignificant planetary system. How much longer are you planning to stay?"

"Until I have stripped everything of value!"

The goddess wasn't sure exactly what Obsidian had in mind, but she was not going to let him scare her any more than he already had.

"If you accept my proposition," she continued, "you will learn the whereabouts of a mysterious new form of electromagnetic power available on planet Mars. It was discovered recently by humans from planet Earth. Or perhaps you simply don't need it? I'm sure you have enough power under your slimy belt. You couldn't possibly want more."

"Tell me! I command you to tell me all about it! Where is it? I want to know! In return, I promise not to eat your sniveling creatures I've taken prisoner." He added under his breath, "Until after I have taken possession of it."

"Not so fast. I'll tell you on one condition. Before you can receive the gift of this power, you must release my twenty-five subjects alive and well on planet Mars! Do you agree to do this?"

Obsidian's black eyes flickered. "And what happens if I don't agree?"

"You'll miss out on the most incredible new discovery in this entire galaxy," she replied. "Eventually you will move on to the next spiral, leading to another galaxy. What a shame, never knowing or possessing the mysterious new power source. Probably just as well. It should be left for someone more worthy than you to take it. What is your decision?"

His beady eyes studied Aphrodite closely. Eventually, after a long silence, Obsidian responded. "All right, I'll accept your proposition. I see that you know much more than I first assumed, goddess. Every world has its own mystery, and it is my job to seek it out and exploit it." However, he was thinking, *I'll go and conquer Mars and afterward I'll return here for the silly goddess. She will be mine!*

Obsidian was so consumed by his greed and the prospect of obtaining a new power source that he snorted again and again, in a mocking gurgle, until the very echo was fatigued from repeating his delight.

Aphrodite kept her word and the warlord left her. He returned to the bridge, giving new orders. "Set the coordinates for Mars! Prepare to leave as soon as possible!"

Alone again, Aphrodite felt rather nervous. She could hardly believe he hadn't tried to kill her or take her prisoner. For some time, she couldn't bring herself to do anything except watch helplessly as brutal warriors formed foul visions of hatred, poking and prodding her frightened, trapped Crystallites. The goddess shuddered to think about what fate might await them as their cage was hauled up the metal ramp and into the ship's underbelly.

The *Zonosor* finally took off. Aphrodite stared blankly at a series of lights stretching along the back of the battleship, now fading into the distance on its way to Mars. She breathed deeply, until she caught a whiff of a putrid smell. A dry, rank odor of death lingered in the air. It caused her to focus now on the horror of the devastation and wretchedness that had befallen her once exquisite planet. Trampled crystal flowers and the still-burning remnants of tiny villages lay scattered upon the terrain that had once been filled with unconditional love.

As the chariot glided aimlessly around, Aphrodite's attention was caught by the entrance to a deep gorge hidden between the mountain ranges. In the eerie light she could just make out a small stream flowing between the boulders that filled the valley beneath her. The rocky overhang formed gigantic shadows, and with the dark clouds that had now gathered overhead, the barren gulf presented a gloomy picture. Although the sight reminded her of the cold-blooded creatures that had butchered her planet, she somehow felt drawn to follow this passage through the mountains.

Flicking the reins, she carefully guided her turtledoves for several miles along the gorge. Finally, it opened out at the edge of Crystal Lake, the largest of the blue lakes on Venus. Barely visible in the dim light, it seemed like the last peaceful place in a barren pit of torment. The silence was almost deafening.

Aphrodite brought the chariot down onto a somewhat level patch of stony ground on the steep mountainside. She leaped out, falling heavily. In her panic, the goddess scrambled up the rocky slope instead of down, her broken sandals slipping on loose stones. She paused for a moment, realizing her mistake. She quickly turned around and ran down toward the water. Thorns in the scattered undergrowth ripped her silken garment and pierced her skin. Blood flowed from the wounds and trickled down her legs.

By the time her trembling body reached the edge of the lake, she collapsed, her hands slipping into the icy water. Small wavelets swirled around her and gently lapped the shore. Feeling abandoned and without a future, Aphrodite began to weep. Exhausted beyond comprehension, the distraught goddess sighed. She straightened up, took one last look around, and then slid into the water.

Aphrodite swam as fast as she could away from the traumatic shoreline and the threat of capture. To her amazement, she found herself surrounded by golden shards of light bursting through the thick clouds above her. She discovered that her body had miraculously transformed into that of a mystical fish. The soft light gently touched her glistening fins and long sweeping tail. Her new form sparkled like a jewel.

When the light began to fade, she slipped silently out of sight into the deep, cold waters of Crystal Lake.

# 9

## *Underbelly*

The interior of the *Zonosor* was a wretched place. Amid all the torment that spun around the twenty-five prisoners like mesh, the younger members of the group withdrew behind a wall of solitude. All sat on low benches of flat metal beams, supported by steel crates. They had never seen anything so horrific, but none could tear their eyes away. The scene was beyond belief.

In front of them sat Rogg, a huge Hadesian guard, perched on a giant metal stool. His forked burgundy tongue flickered feverishly; the only clothing he wore was a grimy piece of cloth, fastened at the waist by a single knot. The fearsome reptilian munched on a leg of rotten meat, ripping at it with serrated teeth while thick saliva dripped onto the floor. Its foul stench forced the captives to lean away.

Onyx felt a low rumble in his stomach. He chose not to stare at Rogg as the Hadesian gnawed on the rancid, meat-laced bone and waved it in their direction. Although the boy was hungry, his appetite quickly disappeared.

"Ugh! Disgusting!" Jade muttered.

Rogg raised the bone in the air, a signal for his subordinates. They were rather slow to respond. Not impressed, he grunted and growled loudly. Four more ferocious reptilians, carrying flaming torches, appeared out of the gloom. The eyes of the Crystallites widened as they saw thick green phlegm dripping from open mouths. Somehow, the prisoners managed to remain composed while the grotesque guards lumbered around, finding wall brackets for their torches.

A strange growl from Rogg encouraged his captives to stay focused. At his command, bags made of loosely woven fabric were slipped over the heads of the prisoners. Some of the Crystallites screamed as the stinking cloth covered their faces and hung limp around their necks. The tall guards bent over their distraught captives and kept a close eye on them. Petite wrists and ankles were bound with heavy shackles. Each prisoner was roughly hauled to his or her feet by one arm; they struggled to stay upright. Several of them cowered as their knees buckled. Every muscle in their shoulders and backs strained.

Rogg spoke in a low, rumbling voice that built to a thunderous shout. "Don't bother screaming, you sniveling little rats! There's no one to help you. We should've eaten you when we had the chance. It's the only way to deal with creatures like you! Now, believe it or not, I've actually been ordered to protect you and keep you safe while we take you through the underbelly on the conveyor belt!" The black slits of his eyes narrowed as he grabbed a torch from the wall; a spurt of flame shot out in their direction. The Crystallites feared for their lives. All sensed they were in grave danger. Finally, as the last prisoner was lifted onto the belt, the guard jerked his thumb upward.

Hematite, standing at the head of the line, was jolted against his heavy chains as the conveyor belt began to move. They produced a jangling sound, and the motion almost caused the elder to topple over. He peered intently through his bag and was just able to make out the figures of his captors. With shoulders hunched, they glared at their prisoners, their mouths curled in wicked smiles.

He was startled when one unexpectedly looked in his direction and growled, "Tell me, Elder. How does Obsidian expect us to make it through this tunnel and keep you lot alive?"

Hematite bravely held the guard's fearful stare through the cloth, wishing he could disappear. He swallowed, then answered warily, "Faith."

The reptilian shoved his ugly face close to Hematite's. His hot, foul breath wafted through the material into the elder's nostrils. Evil black eyes raked over him with hatred. "What faith? Oh, so you think you're a little god too, do you, pathetic, miserable creature! Food, that's what you are! A couple of measly mouthfuls!"

As they traveled further into the bowels of the *Zonosor*, claustrophobia and panic set in. Strange-looking rogue rats scurried away from the flaming torches. Superimposed on the dreadful scene was a putrid odor. The smell was so potent it made the Crystallites feel nauseated. They kept their heads bowed most of the time, staring despondently at the belt. When the prisoners looked sideways, they caught a frightening glimpse of countless depraved eyes staring at them from the darkness.

Eight more enormous prison guards approached the conveyor belt and climbed aboard. The Crystallites heard vulgar, guttural cries of frustration in the distance and whispering voices close by. Their hands trembled. The sound of the whispering voices grew louder, a repugnant sound with no visible source. The tunnel seemed to go on forever.

Dim lights turned into blurred streaks as the belt picked up speed. Rasping sounds echoed throughout the depressing tunnel. The atmosphere was volatile.

Then the belt slowed, and without warning an enormous reptilian form appeared out of the shadows. He lunged with outstretched arms at the moving belt, but the Crystallites were just out of reach.

They were approaching the foundry, a treacherous zone where hundreds of ravenous workers labored in unbelievable heat, melting down tons of iron ore and other metals. Molten ore shot out from nearby furnaces and sprayed the conveyor belt. The Crystallites screamed. Boiling hot steam lined the far side of the tunnel and fierce winds blew, carrying a continual, fiery rain. The prisoners tried to raise their restricted hands in an attempt to shelter one another, but the hot downpour still fell on many, stinging and burning delicate skin.

Hematite tried speaking with the others using telepathy, which distracted him from his gloomy thoughts. In his fatigued mind, he tried to contact Aphrodite but received no response. Despite the elder's courageous attempt to appear calm, his distress was obvious to all.

Many curious, hungry reptilians stopped work and turned to stare greedily, salivating, at the Crystallites. More volatile beasts lunged at them, so Rogg ordered extra guards to climb onto the belt to protect his charges. His orders were to deliver the prisoners safely to the gatekeeper's dungeon, ready for inspection by Obsidian.

Rogg noticed a commotion up ahead and narrowed his eyes. As he came closer, he realized what was happening. His angry voice boomed through the tunnel. The belt slowed to a halt and the senior guard jumped off. He stomped away in the direction of the noisy bunch of workers.

Without authorization, these foolish workers had unlocked several large metal containers filled with bees. Unaware of Rogg's arrival, they were jubilantly smearing the golden goo all over their grimy bodies, thrilled by its flavor. They heard a thunderous roar behind them and froze.

"I demand to know who gave you filthy imbeciles permission to eat the captain's honey? He is going to be absolutely furious!"

One opened his sticky mouth to speak, but Rogg continued to yell. "You rotten, thieving scoundrels! You have work to do! You don't have time to eat! Get back to work before I have you beaten, you good-for-nothing wretches!"

Later, after the news of this crime reached Obsidian, he gave orders for all those guilty to be starved to death in solitary confinement.

Rogg jumped back on board and gave a signal. The belt jerked into life again.

The Crystallites craned their necks and strained their eyes, curious about their surroundings. Above, there appeared to be many levels of varying sizes, each one occupied by hundreds of aggressive-looking Hadesians. Other conveyor belts could be seen beside steep metal staircases leading to higher levels. Some branched off to cover vast floors stretching farther than their eyes could see.

Their belt rounded a sweeping curve and came to a halt as the Crystallites drew level with a metal platform. There was an eerie silence as the guards proceeded to remove the prisoners from the belt. Rogg and the other guards wore a new expression on their faces—a strange mixture of eager anticipation and anxiety. A heavy metal door opening below the platform made a buzzing sound, followed by a click.

The reality of what was happening began to dawn on the Crystallites as they were forced to walk across the platform and descend a set of metal stairs. The guards seemed to have subtly changed, becoming more grotesque and nasty.

The captives were directed through two heavy, wrought-iron gates and into a long, broad corridor. A soulless feeling seeped throughout the depths of the *Zonosor*. The dim light of torches revealed odd blemishes splattered across the gray metal walls. At first glance they looked like brown paint, but closer inspection revealed they were actually dried bloodstains. It was a frightening indication of past abuses inflicted on unknown, hapless prisoners. Gory implements of torture came into view, mounted upon the dark walls.

Fifteen yards down the hall, the Crystallites were led through a solid metal door marked "Gatekeeper." Rogg closed it behind them with a resounding clang, and the bags were roughly removed from their heads. The ordeal of the last few hours had left the captives feeling exhausted. As guards shoved them into line, they stood with eyes closed, heads downcast. Not one of the prisoners could even begin to imagine what was coming next.

Hematite cautiously opened his eyes but kept his gaze on the shackles set tight around bruised and painful ankles. When the elder managed to raise his head, a cold shiver raced up and down his spine. Although the room was dark and dreary, he noticed a formidable pair of ugly iron gates set into one wall. An opening in the floor revealed the top of a spiral staircase. A slight breeze stirred, crooning with a kind of eerie drone. Particles of grime were visible in the rays of dim light from the torches.

In the gloom, something hideous could be seen making its way up the stairs. Upon reaching the top, a large, grotesque reptilian stepped forward and grunted. He sauntered over to the Crystallites with a sadistic grin and tugged at his jaw. Standing directly in front of them, he roared, "I am Lorc, the gatekeeper!"

# 10

## *A Mysterious Object*

The gatekeeper's roar was followed by a taunting chuckle, causing panic in the hearts of the prisoners. In the darkness, Lorc's teeth gleamed like sharp knives; his black eyes had a malevolent shine. The reptilian's short torso was hidden beneath a gray cloak, with a tan-colored cord fastened by an unusual buckle. The oversize buckle had peculiar markings, repugnant to the eye: three coiled snakeheads connected to a rat's backbone. In a gnarled hand, Lorc held a long metal rod. Sparing no thought for hygiene, he scratched at inflamed skin. His body gave off an odor of festering decay.

The Crystallites' eyes were transfixed by the disturbing sight of the gatekeeper as he hobbled back and forth. They knew he was counting down the minutes until he unleashed the fullness of his wrath. It came sooner than expected.

Lorc flicked his fierce tail. In one powerful blow, it lashed out and gave Hematite's shoulder a significant wallop. The elder fell to the ground, gasping for breath. The gatekeeper snorted. He bellowed, "Miserable bits of garbage! You don't deserve to live! I'd like to see you all dead!" Snatching a handful of long ice-white hair, he hauled Hematite sideways across the floor. Hematite's palms were scraped raw, his knees scuffed. Every muscle in his tiny body screamed in agony.

The gatekeeper twisted round and caught sight of Jade. He grinned dangerously at her and then poked the rod into Onyx's stomach, pushing hard. Doubling up in agony, Onyx fell backward and crashed into a guard.

Peridot stepped forward bravely in an attempt to shield his son. Not giving the young father any mercy, the gatekeeper thrashed his tail again and sliced Peridot's cheek with flawless accuracy. Blood ran in rivulets down his face, dripping off his nose and chin. With a ruthless screech, Lorc stopped abruptly in front of the iron gates. He undid the huge metal lock with a giant, rusty key.

As the guards stepped forward, ready to shove the Crystallites through the open gates, Jade shrieked. A door had slid open, and in strode Obsidian, a fearsome vision of malice. The guards stood abruptly to attention. With an almighty screech of rage, the warlord yelled, "Excellent! Lock them up!" The Crystallites feared their lives would come to an end very soon.

Two guards pushed the twenty-five prisoners through the gates and into the dungeon. They entered a dark, dank corridor dimly lit by occasional torches. Uninviting cells were visible on either side through heavy metal bars. One cell gate was unlocked by a guard, and all the prisoners were shoved through into the foul-smelling gloom.

"All counted. Fourteen children, five women, and six men," barked the guard. The Hadesian's face twisted horribly as he gave them a grisly smile and slammed the grill shut. So much hatred emanated from the reptilians' voices that some of the older Crystallites began to be unresponsive to the volatile tones.

Lorc roared, "That'll do now. Leave the stupid wretches alone. They're not going anywhere!"

The captives' spirits lifted a little as the sound of the guards' footsteps became fainter, but their predicament gave them little hope of ever returning to Venus alive.

Hematite exhaled, long and slow, and then leaned back against the rough wall, favoring his injured shoulder. He stretched out his legs. Pins and needles roamed throughout his whole body, jabbing him in one place after another.

An hour later, the elder was still in a stunned state, sitting rigid and uncommunicative. He desperately wanted to sort out the confusion in his mind. How was he going to save his friends from imminent torture or death? What could he say to console them? He closed his eyes for several minutes and finally reached a calmer state of mind. Contact with Aphrodite was his last hope. No words left his lips as he struggled to reach her with his mind.

Meanwhile, Peridot tried not to think about their predicament as he rummaged around in the cold and dark. The more he strained his eyes, though, the less he saw. Then the anxious father glimpsed a snippet of white drawing closer. It was Onyx.

"I don't like that horrible smell," the boy moaned miserably. "It's making me feel sick, Dad."

Peridot peered at the ground and could just make out the bodies of some decomposed rats scattered around. He tried to humor Onyx. "I don't like it either, son. Let's pretend we don't have a nose."

Onyx raised one eyebrow at his father and gave him a

half smile. The boy closed his eyes, kneading his temples, and then wandered back to Topaz.

Except for Peridot, everyone sat on the cold, hard floor and formed a semicircle around Hematite. Their chasm of horror, dark and ghostly, was about twenty feet square. At the sides and back, the floor seemed to merge into the walls. Above them was a filthy, angular ceiling.

Peridot stood alone. His face was battered and bruised. The blood that oozed from his left cheek was finally beginning to congeal. In one corner, not far from where he stood, he noticed a weak glimmer of red light slowly brightening. A mysterious object was becoming visible in the gloom. He narrowed his eyes. Deciding to approach it, he groped around in the dim light. "Ouch!" he cried as he unexpectedly bumped his shin. The object appeared to be an oval-shaped chunk of iron ore.

Placing his hands on the rock, Peridot steadied himself. To his surprise, the strange object felt smooth. He ran his fingers down its sides and then tapped on it. There was a hollow sound. He gathered his thoughts and whispered, "It feels like some kind of metal egg." Peridot alerted the others, inviting them to take a look.

Bixbite, Garnet, and Topaz stood up and managed to find their way to where Peridot stood. They surrounded the object, staring at it curiously.

"What do you suppose it is? Or what's inside it?" Topaz asked her husband. She rubbed it gently with her hand.

"I'm not sure exactly," Peridot replied. "I can feel something over here. Oh, it seems to be a small clasp."

"Maybe it will help us escape. How do we open it?" Bixbite inquired hopefully.

Still leaning his shoulder against the wall for support,

Hematite felt a current of warm air blow across his skin. He was listening to their conversation and answered Bixbite's question. "Maybe we shouldn't try. Whatever is in there could be dangerous. Then again, maybe it's our only hope of escape."

All looked at one another and nodded.

With assistance from Bloodstone, a pretty teenage girl, the injured elder approached the curious object and laid the palm of one hand on it. Opaque, colored energies began to pour from both his hands, spilling over its smooth exterior. It crackled and simmered as the energies trickled down the hard surface like liquid. Next, he placed his ear to the metal and listened, after taking the precaution of asking Bloodstone to keep an eye on the corridor. Onyx and Jade offered to help her.

Bloodstone took hold of the children's hands as they moved into position. No one wanted to arouse the gatekeeper's attention. Lorc was sitting contentedly in a small cave farther down the corridor, devouring decayed rats.

All the adults now examined the iron egg. They placed their hands on it and focused hard, bringing their energies to life. The soothing scent of lavender wafted into the steamy air as hazy energies of pink, blue, and gold covered the rock face. Out of breath, one by one they drew back. Hematite was the last to break contact with the egg. Shrugging, he sat on the grimy floor.

Suddenly there was a screech, followed by the sound of a tail being dragged over a hard metal floor. Heavy footsteps steadily approached their cell. Onyx let out a voiceless scream. "Quick! The gatekeeper is coming!" The three watchers darted back across the floor.

The prisoners dropped to the ground, pretending they

were asleep. Lorc's ugly face peered silently through the bars. Satisfied by what he saw, their jailer twisted round and hobbled back to his lair.

"We really do need to get this thing open!" Hematite whispered urgently.

The adults returned to the egg. Intense energies flowed from them as they placed their small hands on its surface. The dingy cell came to life with a bright mix of color bouncing and crackling from every metal wall.

Topaz was the first to give up, followed by Garnet and the other three women. The men turned around and leaned forward, pushing with their backs against the egg.

Hematite straightened up, his eyes narrowing. Lack of progress sent him into a fit of anger. Taking a deep breath, he clenched his teeth. "I will give it one last shot! If I fail this time, we will have to let it be. We cannot afford to waste any more of our precious energies."

The elder cast an invisible net over the object, summoning every ounce of his power from deep within. The tremendous sensation Hematite felt almost tore him apart; he visualized an explosion with clouds of smoke. It was a struggle to keep his thoughts balanced. Those near him moved away as their elder's body shook. He rocked on his heels, visibly dazed. He blinked several times, staring at them as if they weren't there.

"I didn't know he could do that!" Bixbite whispered to Peridot, who shrugged in reply.

Everyone watching felt as if they were suspended in time. They were all silent, but many pairs of eyes flicked back and forth from Hematite to the object. Nothing happened, absolutely nothing; the egg did not budge. Silence hung in the air, thick and tense.

Topaz moved close to Hematite, straining to pick up any mental feedback. The exhausted elder was slumped over the egg as if he expected it to crack open at any moment.

The gatekeeper's sharp howl echoed through the corridor again, but he didn't make another appearance.

Hematite's eyelashes lightly brushed Topaz's hand. That was all the warning she had before he collapsed on the floor.

Garnet immediately fell to her knees, landing beside Hematite. With quick reflexes, she rolled him onto his back. Then she felt the reassuring hand of Topaz on her shoulder. The two women used telepathy to encourage each other.

Hematite opened his eyes sooner than anticipated. The rest of the Crystallites felt themselves slipping completely into his thoughts; no one resisted. The elder succeeded in erasing the unbearable memories of the last hours from their minds. Feelings of chaos, uncertainty, and dread no longer seized them.

Although the elder had failed to unlock the mysterious object, he still had everyone's trust. Hematite decided to leave the egg alone for now. His energy flowed unconditionally into the others and rapidly healed all their injuries. He filled their hearts with love and courage, leaving them feeling invigorated once more. Each one was reconnected to the light through Hematite's amazing abilities.

Garnet blinked as she found herself staring at Topaz's strange-looking skin. "Why are you looking at me like that, Garnet?" asked Topaz.

There had been no definitive moment of transformation. In the dim light, Topaz glanced round and realized that everyone's appearance had somehow changed. Their bronze skin had turned olive, and their eyes of cerulean blue had become steel gray.

The Crystallites gathered closer together. They were grateful that so far they had survived the dangers lurking within the dungeon, although they still remained in the merciless hands of the gatekeeper. Hematite's acknowledgment of Aphrodite's sacred traditions, along with the foundation she had built over thousands of years, was enabling them to rise above their horrendous situation.

# 11

## *Bloodstone*

The twenty-five Crystallites had been imprisoned on board the battleship for some time when Girmlot and Razil made their way through the upper decks. Keeping pace with one another, the pair approached the first of a series of metal stairs. The officers descended rapidly and headed toward the foundry. At the entrance, they each grabbed a metal rod to protect themselves from the ravenous workers.

"You're going the wrong way! It's this tunnel!" roared Girmlot as he entered a gloomy passage that led to the dungeon. After the commander's many trips back and forth to that wretched place, the route was quite familiar to him.

Torches lining the walls produced pools of amber light, casting huge, flickering shadows. A lengthy passage terminated at an iron door with a fleur-de-lis etched into it.

"This is it!" hissed Girmlot, banging loudly on the door.

Inside, Lorc heard their noise and moved toward the door, making a growling sound. He undid the lock, turned the handle, and pulled the door open. With arms folded across his enormous chest, the gatekeeper stared at them. There was no need for words, only a nod of mutual recognition; they were all aware of their purpose.

"Follow me!" bellowed Lorc, breaking the silence.

At the dungeon's iron gates, the gatekeeper watched dark shadows fall across scaly faces as each officer stepped across the threshold. He passed his torch to Razil before dragging the heavy gates closed with his gnarly hands.

In single file, they stomped down the corridor. Lorc had a large whip in one hand and raised it threateningly at any prisoner who dared stand too close to the bars. The starving reptilian inmates fell backward, squealing. Some took a cut across the face for calling out his name and were left screaming in fits of rage.

The dungeon was full of ear-piercing sounds. As they made their way down the passage, the two officers turned their heads sideways and scowled at prisoners lurking suspiciously within the dark shadows of their confinement. Many of them heckled and quarreled in a chorus of hoarse whispers that seemed to come from everywhere, swirling around and assaulting their ears.

Hematite woke up with a start, his head resting against the cell door. The sour smell of decay was everywhere; the entire prison reeked of it. His befogged mind tried to make sense of the sight of three figures approaching rapidly from the shadows. They were close enough for him to see their serrated teeth in the glow of the torches.

The elder realized with horror that the trio was slowing down. He turned quickly, stricken with fear. His heart was pounding and beads of sweat formed on his wrinkled forehead. Hematite used telepathy to issue an urgent command: *Wake up! At once!* On his hands and knees he crawled toward the others. The footsteps outside grew louder and forced him to crawl faster across the filthy floor.

Almost immediately, three giant silhouettes stood outside the Crystallites' cell. Hematite caught sight of a glint in the gatekeeper's eye and felt there was something sinister behind this visit.

"How m-m-many are there? D-d-do you sense something, Hematite?" stuttered Peridot, his attention darting between the Hadesians and the elder, who had just stepped forward.

Hematite closed his eyes and breathed deeply. He spent a moment in thought before giving Peridot a quick, sharp glance from under his gray eyebrows. The tone of his reply was unusually serious. "There is real danger coming our way. Something dreadful is about to happen."

Peridot didn't utter another sound. He swallowed awkwardly as images of frightening scenarios formed in his mind. Those who overheard their conversation gasped and trembled in fear.

The element of surprise was effective—an unexpected intrusion. The lock fell to the ground with a thud as the officers' torches flared brightly.

Seconds later, startled gray eyes adjusted to the glare. "I can hear you breathing," growled Girmlot in a low, husky voice as he crept toward a small family of three, huddled together some little way from the others. Bloodstone's parents, Aragonite and Galena, shuddered at the sound of his every footstep. The bones of dead rodents crunched beneath giant feet.

Aragonite put one hand on Galena's arm and the other on Bloodstone's shoulder. For a moment they decided to stay put; he gestured for them to crouch down in the corner. As

Aragonite raised a finger to his lips, he heard something scurry away. He gasped when he realized that Lorc was also closing in on them and had heard the noise too. A flaming torch was swiped in front of their faces. Aragonite tried to jump to his feet but stumbled and fell to the floor.

An orange flame shot up. Galena could hardly see in the glaring light. Lorc reached over and hit her with great force. She let go of Bloodstone's hand as her body flew backward, and her head smacked the ground. The reptilian laughed ominously and turned around, heading toward the others.

Jade realized with horror that an evil flare was now closing in on her. Overwhelmed by fear and panic, she raced away toward Bloodstone. Lorc was fascinated by the tiny, two-legged creature and gave chase.

Bloodstone screamed out, "Run, Jade! The beast is behind you!"

Lorc moved swiftly across the floor, keeping his beady eyes fixed on Jade. Within seconds, an outstretched hand grabbed a fistful of ice-white curls and pulled her head around to face him. The child squealed in pain. Frozen with terror, she was mesmerized as he flicked his tongue back and forth excitedly, dribbling horribly.

Bixbite ran toward the attacker. He screamed, "Let her go! Get away from my daughter, hideous creature!"

Lorc glowered. He smiled dangerously at Bixbite, then caught sight of Bloodstone standing close behind him. She shouted loudly in her high-pitched voice, "No! Take me instead! Let Jade go! She is far too young, beast!"

"No, Bloodstone! You can't sacrifice yourself! It's not right!" cried Jade. Tears streamed down her face.

Lorc released his grip on Jade and turned to Girmlot. "I think I've found the one you seek!"

"Our demanding captain will be pleased! Seize her!" he barked in reply.

Hematite and the other adults stared at Bloodstone, keenly aware of her vulnerability. Their eyes held a look of terror. Lorc's razor-sharp claws swatted furiously at Bixbite's upper body, knocking him to the ground. The Crystallite tried in vain to clamber to his feet, but his pain was unbearable.

Topaz couldn't bear to look as Lorc reached down and grabbed Bloodstone's frail arm in a monstrous grip. Peridot and Hematite were unable to tear their eyes away from his malicious smile. They realized in dismay the teenager had no chance of escape; heavy shackles were quickly secured tight around her thin ankles.

A sharp pain jabbed her father's heart as the hideous gatekeeper dragged her by the arm. Aragonite let out a bloodcurdling scream: "Nooooooo!"

"This one's a fighter!" hissed Lorc, twisting his head round toward Razil.

Bloodstone took a deep breath. The light from Razil's torch illuminated her small frame. A shudder of horror rushed through her body as she watched a dangerous smile spread across Lorc's malevolent face.

Girmlot closed in on Bloodstone. A low hissing sound came from his slightly open mouth as his forked tongue slipped in and out. His nostrils flared with each raspy breath. The commander's expression didn't alter, but his black, beady eyes looked her up and down.

"Take her and let's go!" he snorted.

Seconds later the door slammed shut. Dragging Bloodstone between them, kicking and screaming, the three reptilians disappeared down the tunnel.

Aragonite, devastated and despondent, knelt beside his unconscious wife. His heart pounded like a hammer. Through his tears, he used telepathy to follow Bloodstone's quivering shadow while he also lovingly monitored Galena's breathing. Realizing he might very possibly lose the two he loved more than life itself, Aragonite bowed his head. He clenched his fists tightly in the folds of Galena's tattered garment. All color had drained from his cheeks.

Galena stirred and slowly began to wake up. With blurred vision she gazed at her husband and was horror-struck by the grief in his eyes. She glanced about hastily and noticed Bloodstone was missing. A howl of anguish came from her lips as she realized her precious daughter had been taken.

Blood rushed to her head and tears filled her eyes. Galena turned and gagged near the wall, bile spewing from her mouth, her gray face just visible in the warm glow from the torch in the corridor. Noticing that her blood was smeared over the floor in clots and puddles, mixing with her vomit, she gagged again.

# 12

## *Chalice of Taybue*

Bloodstone awoke in solitary confinement, chained to the wall in another cell. It was hot, so hot that it was hard to breathe, and the stench was stupefying. Every breath seemed as if it would be her last. Her eyes felt as though they were going to explode. She struggled to tug on her raggedy dress and managed to pull part of it up to fan her face, but the effort was futile. There was no relief from the oven-like heat.

"Where am I?" Bloodstone muttered. She glanced around her cramped, acrid prison cell. Dozing off again, she tossed and turned, scarcely getting any rest between the shrieks that split the air. In the dull gloom, confined also by the darkness of her foreboding, she felt as though this terrifying ordeal was another horrific nightmare.

Bloodstone's wrists were red-raw, the skin bruised and chafed. She sat up, face pinched, skin pale, and eyes sunken, a ghostlike figure. Running her fingers over the dirty floor, she grasped at tiny shards of scrap metal that were scattered around. Minutes later, she released them from her loose grip.

The girl felt a hopelessness seep into her soul. It took all her strength to calm the terror that surged through her veins.

Light from a flickering torch appeared outside her cell, causing the iron bars to glint. Distorted, shadowy forms moved toward the door. It was shaken with a force that sent a shudder through Bloodstone's body.

Ligwa and Morl, two reptilian guards, emerged from the gloom. Ligwa grabbed the keys fastened to his plaited rope belt and undid the lock. His slanted jaw stuck out, and his eyes peered over the waves of heat produced by the auburn flames.

As he shuffled into the cell, Bloodstone pivoted her head and closed her eyes for a few moments, trying to protect them from the brightness. Frightened by the torchlight, she breathed rapidly and deeply, trying to calm herself. When she opened her eyes, she felt like screaming.

Next, Morl entered the cell. With a clawed hand, he swiped at Bloodstone in a wide, careless swing that gave her just enough time to roll clear. Irritated and cursing loudly, he glared at the girl with a ferocious, doglike gleam in his eyes. As he reached for her small arm, his ugly face was visible in the orange glow. With his other hand, the guard grabbed her heavy chain, which was fastened to the wall with a curved hook. He jerked it so hard that it came right out of the wall, just missing Bloodstone's head.

The reptilian's beady eyes flickered. Two rows of sharp teeth were visible behind thin lips as he snarled, "Get up, wretch! The first item on today's agenda is a very special ceremony, a sacrifice! Yours! You can't be late for that, can you? Horlotha, Obsidian's high priest, will be officiating, and we daren't keep him waiting!" Morl spoke in a husky growl, his voice echoing around the cell like an erratic whisper.

Bloodstone was stunned! Hauling her to her feet, he dragged the girl through the doorway.

Smoke from the torches curled upward as Morl shoved his prisoner into the gloomy passage. Ligwa slammed the metal gate shut. Bloodstone sobbed, shaking uncontrollably. She limped along between the two guards with eyes fixed on the floor, fighting back her tears in vain. Morl struck the girl's bony shoulder with his clenched fist, startling her already distraught nerves. "Shut up, miserable wretch!" She groaned in pain as she staggered along.

They walked faster and turned a corner at the end of the passageway. Hanging loosely on the endless walls was a line of torn banners. The guards chortled, recalling how these had once belonged to their rivals.

The next corridor they entered was dark and tapered. At the end was a solid iron gate, set between two gold pillars, ten feet tall. In its center was a winged sun, a symbol of power and authority. Morl spun around on a clawed foot, snorting hard. He glanced at his cohort, nodding to indicate that they were nearing their destination.

"Stand against that wall!" Morl barked, shoving their captive back. His gnarled knuckles rapped three times in the middle of the winged sun. He paused; at his sides, his hands were balled into tight fists. Bloodstone tried to swallow, but her throat was rigid with terror. She waited, wondering if these would be the last breaths she took.

Finally, the gate groaned on its hinges as it was pulled open. At the threshold, the gatekeeper blocked her view into the gloom on the other side. He hissed a curse and lunged at her with great speed, grabbing her upper arm. The edges of her mouth flinched and she inhaled sharply. He sensed a jolt of adrenaline shoot through her bloodstream and snickered.

His sharp, chilled stare was fixed on her as he released his grip and closed the gate behind the guards. They grabbed hold of their prisoner again, and the three of them advanced slowly through a cavernous chamber. Bloodstone was too overcome with despair to look around, even though she could hear noises. Heavy footsteps reverberated and gruff voices murmured.

They made their way across an open area and descended a flight of stairs leading deeper into the *Zonosor*. The unpleasant odor of iron ore no longer invaded Bloodstone's nostrils, but the heat was increasing. Panic welled up inside her, as her mind replayed the words about a ceremony and a sacrifice.

At the bottom of the stairs was a long hallway with metal doors evenly spaced along it. As she passed each door, the hairs on the back of her neck stood on end and her palms became clammy. An uncontrolled shudder rocked her thin body. Bloodstone recovered and flicked a glance from side to side, but there was nothing to be seen except the guards' shadows creeping along the walls.

"Who or what is behind those doors?" she questioned in a hoarse whisper.

"Silence! Shut up and keep moving!" shouted Ligwa, pushing her roughly.

Finally, after walking down yet another corridor, they passed through a metal door with a large window in the top. The door led into a short hallway with a burning torch hanging on the wall. Its glimmering flame cast an eerie glow on a massive, reptilian, godlike statue made of pewter. The hallway opened out into a courtyard that was teeming with reptilian officers bustling about.

Weaving their way through, the trio reached the

entrance to a hypostyle hall. The front was adorned with pomegranates and flanked by two columns. These were the pillars of the reptilian gods of dawning light, symbolizing severity and mercy. Dozens of lofty gold pillars supported the high ceiling, and checkered tiles covered the floor.

As she was led into the chamber, Bloodstone began to realize she was in a pagan temple, a place of ceremonial worship. At the far end, there was a large altar set on top of a dais. It was made of pewter, with ornate designs decorating its sides. In the center, a fire was burning in an enormous pit. Apart from the distant hum of the *Zonosor*'s engines and the crackling of the fire, silence seemed to settle in the cavern like a heavy blanket.

Obsidian was briefly visible stomping through the murky shadows; then he appeared to be consumed by them and vanished into the darkness. As the guards waited for their leader to reappear, the silence intensified along with the unrelenting heat.

Footsteps echoed around the chamber. Morl, looming over Bloodstone, reached out and caught her left arm in his right hand. He gripped it tightly, very tightly. As he glanced down at her, his jaws gaping, dribbles of putrid saliva trickled from his forked tongue. The girl spun round in shock and whimpered. Looking up at him, his victim slowly sank to her knees with no attempt to struggle. She let out a frenzied screech as his clawed hands hauled her upward. Bloodstone found herself staring into his cold, piercing eyes. Morl leered, lifting her even higher. For a moment, she thought her oppressor was going to strike her. Bloodstone's face turned gray; she breathed deeply, trembling in fear.

At that moment, Obsidian sailed out of the shadows. His expression darkened. He waved his clenched fists in the air and shrieked, "I want that creature alive! Bring her to me now, you imbecile!"

The warlord's words sent chills up and down the captive's spine. As the cowering guard hastened to obey, Obsidian glared fiercely at him and shone a torch in Bloodstone's face to ensure she was unharmed. Satisfied, the warlord turned toward the dais. His dark gray cloak swept out momentarily and revealed the weapons attached to his belt. To her dismay, the girl caught a glimpse of a gleaming sword.

Holding Bloodstone aloft like a trophy, Morl followed his master toward the dais, his long, serpent like tongue flicking as he shook his head feverishly. He opened his clawed hands, letting her fall with a thud in front of the dais. His task completed, the guard slunk away into the shadows.

Dressed in the torn rags that had once been pure white, Bloodstone had finally reached the depths of despair. Her tormented mind was fully occupied with what might happen next. She had come to understand that exchanging her life for Jade's was her fate—her legacy for the remaining twenty-four survivors from Venus.

The girl was almost paralyzed with fear. The tiles felt painfully hard beneath her aching body. She raised her head a little. Then her stomach lurched, bile rising into her throat. What was the Chalice of Taybue doing, sitting on top of this pagan altar? Somehow Obsidian must have found Aphrodite's precious cup and stolen it!

The chalice was made of clear crystal, cut in such a delicate fashion that it sparkled, even in dim light. On the outside was a jewel set into a gold pentacle; feet of burnished gold supported the stem. Bloodstone had seen the goddess use the cup only at very special ceremonies. On these occasions it was filled with a pale bronze liquid made with

Elderflower Elixir, powdered pearls, and consecrated water from Crystal Lake. It now appeared that the warlord had not only discovered Aphrodite's sacred recipe, but he had managed to steal the ingredients too! Anger and fear rose up inside her.

Beside the chalice, wisps of aromatic smoke rose from a pewter dish, forming an image of a black butterfly. Inside the dish was burning a mixture of powdered gold, frankincense, and myrrh. Also on the altar was a thin black case.

Summoning her remaining courage, Bloodstone glanced to the right and spied a reptilian standing behind the altar. His appearance was different from most of the others, but he was of a similar height to Lorc, the gatekeeper. He wore a maroon cape fastened at the neck by an ornate sun-shaped clasp, the rest of his body being unclothed. The beast had very dark brown, almost black, scaly skin that looked impenetrable, like armor. It was coarse and somewhat glossy, with significant protrusions. His demeanor was decidedly smug. The girl sensed he was a dark high priest.

Turning her eyes toward Obsidian, she cowered in shock and repulsion. He was now seated on a bench on the dais, with his legs spread apart. He was joined by Horlotha. Bloodstone found she had just enough strength to listen, via telepathy, to the whispered conversation between the evil creatures.

With a wild raucous laugh, the warlord stood up. He bellowed, "Let the ceremony begin!"

Scores of reptilian officers swarmed into the temple in eager anticipation. A hush fell over the assembly as Obsidian and Horlotha moved into position. They stood on the dais in front of the altar, clawed hands folded in the creased fabric of their cloaks. The aroma from the incense wafting through the chamber was accentuated by the heat in the air. It caused forked, burgundy tongues to flick in and out feverishly.

Behind the altar, large screens slid open, revealing an expansive view of the heavenly constellations through the *Zonosor*'s windows. Dominating the panorama was the Black Sun, its glowing corona creating a mystical setting suitable for a ceremony of sacrifice. A single shard of silver light bounced off the tiled floor. Violently vibrant and packed with more energy than rays from the true sun, this dark spiritual light produced a powerful surge of bloodthirstiness in the warlord and his high priest.

They waited anxiously for a short time. A piercing, empowering beam struck the rim of the chalice. As it touched the potion, the silence was split by a sharp crack, loud and close. A spark shot up and floated like a feather on a breath of warm air.

Horlotha grinned with sadistic pleasure, his nostrils flaring. He leaned over the chalice, admiring the exquisitely beautiful reflection of the dark sun in the bronze liquid. As the priest continued to peer intently into the cup, he received a vision, a revelation of the spiritual structure of the solar system and the relationships between the gods. It was almost time.

Meanwhile, Bloodstone stared into the untamed flames of the fire, transfixed. A whispering voice wove its way into her consciousness. She became aware that Aphrodite was trying to communicate with her from the depths of Crystal Lake.

*"Your death shall not be in vain. The legacy you leave will follow the Crystallites throughout all eternity, dear Bloodstone."* The goddess's voice was inspirational and had a ring of truth.

Aphrodite directed the girl's eyes to the pentacle set in the chalice and instructed her to focus intently upon the jewel. As Bloodstone obeyed, the pentacle grew brighter, producing its own beam of light. Thin rays of crimson drifted across the gloom, illuminating her mind. The light unlocked a powerful gift in her: the ability to create a crystal prism inside her mind. She felt an overwhelming sense of calmness and an ability to accept the horrendous event about to occur.

Inside Bloodstone's mental prism, the goddess began to weave a textured veil, brighter than sunlight. Enfolded within it, Bloodstone saw Aphrodite's last remaining children. Although in reality they were still in danger in the dungeon of the *Zonosor*, the girl saw only beauty through the veil. Her visions predicted that these Crystallites would become strong and somehow be sustained through all their pain and suffering.

Bloodstone closed her eyes, entering into a state of meditation. As the apparitions grew clearer, she felt empowered.

*"Dear child,"* whispered Aphrodite urgently, her voice becoming faint. *"I am relying on you to send a plea for help to Zeus and Ares. Unless they come to the aid of your family and friends, they are all doomed!"*

Without hesitation, Bloodstone obeyed, repeating the names of the twenty-four Crystallites in her exhausted mind and begging the gods to help them escape.

Sensing that the atmosphere in the temple was becoming boisterous, Bloodstone opened her eyes and caught her breath. Her long, dirty hair hung in strings, and her face was still damp from her tears. For a moment she remained motionless as a dark shadow drifted across her tiny frame.

She looked up and saw the priest standing over her. In her trancelike state, she heard his guffaw of laughter, followed by an energetic vocal outburst in a strange, primordial dialect.

He dragged her up onto the dais and pulled her to her feet. The air surrounding her shimmered with red. In the dim light, she flicked a glance at her bruised wrists, encircled by shackles. Horlotha grabbed her roughly under the chin, forcing his victim to look into his face. His eyes darkened as he heaved her up onto the altar.

"Aphrodite no longer lives! The secret of immortality belongs to Obsidian!" The hiss in the priest's voice resonated throughout the temple, echoing off the metal walls. The eager reptilians responded and stomped their feet in a demanding rhythm, impatient for the sacrifice to begin.

In front of the crowd, Horlotha held up a clawed hand, signaling for silence again. In one smooth, practiced movement, he picked up the thin black case and pulled out a glistening sword. Holding it above his head in triumph, he chanted again in the unknown dialect. The light beam from the dark sun rebounded across the floor, fractured by the blade of the sword.

Bloodstone inhaled deeply. Here in the conqueror's temple, lying on an altar in the presence of his dark high priest, she was absolutely defenseless. There was nothing she could do to protect herself. The situation was too difficult for her innocent young mind to process. Paralyzed by fear now, she became mesmerized by Horlotha's voice, deep and powerful, as he repeated over and over, "The secret of immortality belongs to Obsidian!"

Still chanting ardently, his sword flashing in the ray of light, the priest lunged forward. The blade pierced Bloodstone's heart, drawing blood. Her shriek of pain resonated throughout the temple. The vile creature hissed again, his yellow eyes expanding with rage as he withdrew the sword, snarling. Then he spun around and raised the bloody sword over the altar. In one sweeping arc, he carefully lowered the tip into the Chalice of Taybue. At the same time, Horlotha felt an unexpected surge of power through the sword, distracting him momentarily.

Obsidian, who had been watching closely, exhaled loudly with excitement and exaltation. He turned to face the throng and hissed, "Success! The secret of immortality is now mine! Forever!"

Setting the sword down on the altar, Horlotha faced Obsidian and raised his hands. His voice once again resonated inside the temple. "None but you, oh great warlord, holds the secret of eternal life, and this secret will be all yours forever!"

Bloodstone lay still on the altar, her body curled up like a fetus, her jaw open. She gasped for one more breath with her last remaining ounce of strength. Her bloodstained hands clasped at the fatal wound in her chest. The victim's shrieks were now so faint they were barely audible. With her eyes glazed over from excruciating pain, the last sight she saw was the interior of an alien temple teeming with ferocious bestiality.

Bloodstone only lasted a few minutes more, fighting for her life with frenzied desperation. Her body was drenched in the warm red blood oozing from her open wound. It ran down off the surface of the altar and pooled on the dais. Her final breath came in a small, painful gasp, tears blinding her eyes. Release at last!

Ignoring Bloodstone's lifeless body, Obsidian peered into the Chalice of Taybue. The curdling blood was turning the liquid from bronze to rose gold. After gazing at it in wonder, he stepped off the dais and stomped across the hall.

On a shelf in the shadow of a pillar stood a crystal decanter, a large, ornate vessel in which the warlord kept some special herbs. He grabbed it, his long claws scraping the crystal, and returned to the altar. With assistance from Horlotha, he removed the crystal stopper and poured the contents of the chalice into the decanter. After the stopper was pushed back in firmly, the priest placed the decanter beside the empty chalice.

Once this task was completed, Obsidian and Horlotha turned their attention to the body of their victim. A guard was summoned to remove the corpse and to place it in the first chamber down in the hold. This was the one where Aphrodite's birds and animals were confined. It also happened to be directly underneath the temple.

\*\*\*

Meanwhile, back in the Crystallites' cell, Aragonite let out a cry of intense pain. "Something unspeakably dreadful has happened to Bloodstone! I can feel it!" The distraught father's head was cupped in his small hands, and his puny shoulders shuddered convulsively as he knelt on the hard ground. A lock of ice-white hair drooped over his short, thin fingers. Placing his head on Galena's chest, he gently cradled his wife's petite frame in his arms. They clung to each other for a long time, crying and rocking back and forth. Finally, their sobbing faded into desolate whimpers.

Hematite wanted desperately to console the grieving couple. Using telepathy, he asked everyone else to encircle them, holding hands. He knelt down with Aragonite and

Galena and wrapped his arms around the pair, squeezing gently. They leaned into him, longing for comfort. Through their almost overwhelming grief, Bloodstone's parents felt sincere love flow from their friends as every one of them mourned the loss of their beautiful daughter.

Several hours later, many were still awake when someone happened to glance upward. "Look! Up on the ceiling! Where's that strange glow coming from?"

"What's going on?"

"Who's this?"

Questions came thick and fast as an apparition, the size and shape of a teenager, began to form on the far side of the cell. The apparition consisted of brilliant autumn tones: shades of copper, gold and crimson.

"These … were … my daughter's … favorite colors," whispered Galena, almost too afraid to speak.

The figure was surrounded by an aura of bright yellow and soft green, the colors merging smoothly, spilling onto the floor. Within seconds, the floor was covered in thick layers of mist. A strange calmness enveloped them all.

Silence reigned in their cell as the Crystallites gazed on the unexpected, ghostly appearance of Bloodstone. She spoke in a soft, soothing whisper, her words reminding them of her altruism. "There is no greater privilege than to perform an act of selflessness, and no greater honor than to be able to lay down your life for your friends. I hope my willing sacrifice will ultimately save the lives of others. Remember, no one ever walks alone." The apparition faded, along with the feeling of calm.

As they tried to blink back the darkness, the Crystallites were in shock. Some had trouble settling down again after such a strange encounter. The unusual atmosphere made it difficult for them to find comfort in the diminishing sound of her voice.

Completely exhausted, Galena lay on the floor and placed her pounding head on her husband's shoulder. Weeping again, she eventually cried herself to sleep.

# 13

## *Celebration Feast*

*B*ehind a set of golden pillars in the *Zonosor*'s main chamber was a great hall, where final preparations were being made for a banquet. An enormous fire pit dominated the center. Decorative oil lamps hung from Gothic-style beams; statues stood guard around the walls. Expansive iron tables held large, jeweled bowls of exotic fruit and aromatic herbs. In between the bowls sat metal cages crammed with an assortment of live creatures, retrieved from their prison in the first chamber in the hold, squeaking and squealing. Pitchers of warm, fresh blood were being filled from large vats by reptilian servants, as hungry officers filed in and took their seats.

Obsidian strode in. His warriors, arrayed in their finest dress armor, stood to attention. The captain bellowed, "Sit down! Sit down! Eat your fill in preparation for our next battle, and let us also celebrate our success!"

The captain had such confidence in the abilities of all his soldiers that it was his custom to have a victory celebration before a battle. The officers cheered loudly and began at once to gorge themselves, while Obsidian proceeded to take his seat at the head of the top table.

The warlord grinned as he watched servants scurry around, carrying giant-size bowls overflowing with interestingly shaped intestines. He took an evil delight in watching his soldiers hungrily devour live animals. They would often swallow a small creature whole. Larger ones could be seen wiggling between sharp teeth as greedy Hadesians stripped meat off bone, washing it down with mouthfuls of blood from pewter goblets. The servants had a hard time keeping the pitchers topped up.

Soon Obsidian was oblivious to those around him. He became completely engrossed in satisfying his own gruesome appetite, noisily consuming any hapless animal that caught his eye, and quenching his thirst with great gulps of blood. *Ah! Sheer pleasure*, he thought, making a childlike crooning sound. The pitch of his voice deepened to a low groan, though, as he pried a bone out of his gum and wiped his mouth with the back of his hand.

The warlord's attention was grabbed by a figure now appearing at the entrance to the hall. It was Horlotha, who was carefully carrying the crystal decanter from the temple. The priest was followed by several temple servants bearing gifts for Obsidian. The captain had no interest in these trinkets; instead, his greedy eyes were transfixed by the object that held the promise of fulfillment of all his hopes and dreams. He watched it being placed on top of an ancient treasure chest.

Obsidian's nostrils flared as his eyes focused on the decanter's long, slender neck, decorated with fine bands of golden cord. Impatient, he could not help himself. He leaped out of his chair and hurried across the chamber toward it.

As he passed by, several curious officers raised their heads, twisting round to watch the warlord stomp past.

A strange hush descended throughout the great hall, a silence so intense that only the sound of breathing could be heard. Horlotha attempted to present his gifts to Obsidian: decorative fur coats and a spectacular selection of necklaces made from the teeth of exotic animals from conquered planets. However, the warlord brushed him aside as he reached for the decanter. In a single swift motion, he scooped up the vessel and strode back to his seat.

Standing in front of his table, Obsidian held the decanter up to the light and admired its exquisite beauty. All eyes were on the captain. The muscles in his jaw tightened as he removed the stopper and inhaled deeply. The potency of the aroma caused him to take a step backward. He replaced the stopper. Then, gripping it tightly in two clawed hands, Obsidian raised the vessel above his head and hissed Aphrodite's name. The sound echoed around the hall like a slithering serpent.

"Drinking from this decanter will bring me the gift of immortality! No one deserves it more than I do! I have the most brilliant military mind in the entire universe! My expertise on the battlefield has been aptly demonstrated by my many victories in the most vicious kind of combat.

"Soon we will land on our next planet, Mars. We will wield invincible power, with no concern for justice or life—except our own, of course! My army will sweep over the planet like a plague. No force will be able to stand against us. Our hands will drip with blood.

"Listen carefully, fellow warriors! Your main job is to locate the extraordinary electromagnetic power source. While you are doing that, you will strike terror among those who resist. Destroy their sacred places of worship and build me my own shrine, where I will display a special sacred skull. I will outlaw all their gods and deny the inhabitants their right to worship them. Then I will keep all in submission to me, as the conqueror of Mars! It will all be mine!"

A boisterous cheer erupted at full volume. Obsidian pompously returned their salute and signaled for them to carry on with their pre-battle ceremonial feast. He carefully replaced the decanter, with its precious liquid, on the top of the chest.

*** 

Down in the hold, the reptilian guards were cruel; they constantly bickered and fought among themselves. Their politics were far less complicated than those among Obsidian and his officers. Arguments here were won by brute force, not by negotiation. They hated the guards from the higher decks and took any opportunity to pick a fight. Sliv, Slod, and Slig were on duty in the fifth chamber when Ligwa and Morl approached with Bloodstone's corpse.

This large, dimly lit room was filled with all the birds, bees, and other animals captured on Venus. They were crammed into cages of varying sizes that were stacked five high around the walls. One cage on the top level held a number of Aphrodite's turtledoves. They were squashed together, one on top of the other, so that the bodies of those underneath ached from supporting the weight of the ones above.

During the sacrificial ceremony in the temple above their prison, the birds had felt the power of the Chalice of Taybue. Sporadic flashes of light had seeped through tiny cracks between the floor tiles. They had also heard some of the grisly proceedings. When it was all over, the feathered creatures remained traumatized.

There was a loud rapping on the door of the chamber. Sliv slowly shuffled over to open the door.

"Imbeciles! What are you doing down here? Have you been demoted?" sneered Sliv, shaking a clawed fist at Ligwa and Morl.

"Mind your language, despicable rat! We're here on the captain's orders, that's what, so shut up!" Ligwa replied, waving a scaly arm in Sliv's face as he stepped into the chamber. Morl followed, carrying Bloodstone's limp body. As the pair passed by the turtledoves' cage, the birds looked on in trepidation and struggled to keep silent.

"Just drop her and leave!" snarled Slod. The girl's tiny frame, bloodied and lifeless, was dumped onto the floor near the turtledoves and landed with a thump. Ligwa and Morl turned and stomped off, with no regard for the body they had just delivered. Sliv slammed the door hard after them.

All the animals now wore petrified expressions on their faces. There were several hundred creatures in the chamber, but not one of them seemed to be moving. It was impossibly quiet, as if someone had just called for a moment of silence.

Dumbstruck, the turtledoves stared, unable to do anything but gape at the girl's body. They were alarmed at the sight of the fatal wound carved into her tiny frame and were shocked to see that her blood had been completely drained, the final result of a barbaric sacrifice. Those who had known her in life had the most trouble absorbing the horrendous sight.

Several turtledoves slowly began to recover, crooning mournfully. An older bird was the first to speak. "Please, I know you're all devastated by Bloodstone's murder, but we must remain silent. Our lives are in real danger. I think it is time you heard about Aphrodite's plan, though."

The turtledove continued in a hushed voice, "Aphrodite always says how important it is to learn from others' mistakes. She told me about Kronos, the king of the Titans, who stole the sea gods' Cauldron of Pisces. It contained sacred water with life-renewing powers. Kronos didn't care that the sea gods would lose their powers if they could no longer drink their renewal potion. His plan was to gain power for himself by drinking this water."

"That's awful! You're supposed to calm us, not make us feel worse," snapped a young dove trapped at the bottom of the cage.

"Let me finish," the older bird replied patiently. "After learning about the sea gods' experience, our wise goddess put a powerful secret ingredient into her Elderberry Elixir. Obsidian meddles in things he doesn't understand, and he has evil plans for our solar system. His desire is to cause an enormous tempest that will tear it asunder from within. But a long time ago, I overheard Aphrodite speaking with Zeus about the possibility of someone stealing the elixir and maybe even daring to tamper with it. In her wisdom, our goddess has seen to it that anyone interfering with it will suffer severe consequences!"

Right at that moment, Sliv shuffled past on patrol and heard the turtledoves' low chirrups. His beady eyes darted around the chamber. Then he spun round on his clawed foot and lunged forward. Raising a powerful arm, Sliv brought it down hard on the bars of the turtledoves' cage. The birds began to screech loudly. He pushed his gnarled hand through the mangled iron and grabbed a trembling dove. With his fist tightly clenched, the guard glared at the bird for a moment before he quickly wrung its neck.

The others froze, each one afraid that they might be next. They attempted to compose themselves but could not erase a look of dread from their tiny faces.

Sliv laughed raucously as Slod appeared, curious about the noise. With a quick swipe, Slod snatched up the dead bird. "Better get rid of the evidence," he explained, gulping it down and nodding his ugly head. "It's a good thing the captain isn't around. He wouldn't be happy to hear that one of Aphrodite's precious doves has gone missing. Any mention of this and I'll eat you too," he growled, glaring at Sliv.

Slig had been napping in a dark corner, but now he appeared on the scene, disturbed by the racket. He leaned on his gray staff, narrowed his eyes, and then began marching up and down in front of the cages. Several doves shook with fear as he raised a clenched fist, smashing it down on their cage. The cries from the terrified birds sounded like a madwoman's high-pitched squeal. The white rabbits, in a cage below the doves, buried their heads in deep despair. Beneath the rabbits, the bluebirds could no longer sing sweet, honeyed tunes, their throats choked with fright. Slig chided the rabbits and bluebirds for their silence. He tormented them by repeatedly striking their cages.

\*\*\*

When the celebration feast ended, Obsidian retired to his private quarters, and the others returned to their assigned duties. Some of the senior officers assembled to review the battle plans. They gathered in an upper chamber from which they could see the spacecraft's spiked tip.

Girmlot and Razil shuffled off to the bridge. Through an open internal window, the commander watched as hundreds of troopers mobilized in the parade area, preparing for a war march into the battle zone on landing. He was pleased with a lieutenant's harsh tone in speaking to the communications squad, ensuring they understood the importance of keeping in contact with the *Zonosor* once the troops reached their positions.

Girmlot heard a slight click as the door began to open very slowly. Finally, an ensign stepped forward hesitantly, saluted, and stood to attention.

The commander bellowed in a hostile tone, "Ensign, why aren't you with your warriors?"

"I thought I should warn you about a faceless life-form that's supposed to lurk within the depths of Mars. It could pose a threat to us."

There was a long silence, a hacking cough, then more silence. "Whatever you think they are, they don't exist. A mere tale, a stupid rumor!" snarled Girmlot finally. The ensign frowned.

"Get out of my sight!" roared Girmlot. "And don't you dare come here again uninvited and spouting nonsense!"

The ensign hurried away. A few minutes later, Razil left the bridge too, ignoring a contemptuous glare from the commander. He hurried nervously down the foul-smelling corridor to the chamber where the senior officers were meeting. The lieutenant commander arrived just in time to catch the tail end of their heated conversation.

"I've heard that this army is supposed to be extremely fierce, and anyone who threatens to disrupt their planet will be dealt with brutally! Not a lot is known about these mysterious creatures, but they are said to be red."

After Razil left the bridge, Girmlot headed off to Obsidian's quarters. On the way, he caught up with his subordinate and hissed aggressively, "Lieutenant Commander, go back to your post immediately!" Razil saluted and returned to the bridge, his every step heavy and pounding.

Obsidian was sipping a large goblet of fresh blood while he eyed the Elderberry Elixir on a table beside him. He was considering taking his first sip of the elixir when the commander's loud knock interrupted him. Rising to his feet, the warlord wandered over to the corner of his chamber, jerked his head back, and roared, "Who is it?"

The commander entered. "We're approximately eight million miles from Mars and will arrive within a couple of hours. What do you want me to do with the prisoners?"

The warlord's fierce voice grew deeper. "Let those sniveling beings watch me take possession of Mars, and then we'll eat them!"

# 14

## *Apparition*

As they slept, the Crystallites all had the same powerful dream, one so realistic that it was impossible for them to forget. At first, a cold fear gripped the hearts of Bloodstone's parents. They saw their daughter standing in the center of a dark chamber and surrounded by caged animals. But once her apparition began to speak, comforting feelings of love and trust filled them with hope.

Bloodstone's voice, full of power and authority, was as smooth as velvet. She spoke first of Obsidian's desire to become immortal. Scenes Aphrodite had enabled Bloodstone to see in the temple's fire flowed into their exhausted minds.

"A secret red army, an ancient force, is observing Obsidian and his warriors. This army will rise in your favor and move silently among the enemy, providing you with a path that will penetrate the veil and lead you toward the light."

As the full weight of Bloodstone's words simultaneously entered each one's consciousness, the Crystallites gasped in unison and woke up. They inhaled deeply, and then on exhaling, their initial sense of optimism faded. Although there had been a comforting gleam in the girl's eyes, they were left with an ache piercing their minds and hearts.

"No!" screamed Jade, feeling an unspeakable horror fill her tiny body when her honorable friend's apparition disappeared. The young girl's fears of the future began to fade, though, as a pure and wondrous light filled her heart.

In the distance, the Crystallites heard the sound of clawed feet, a heavy shuffle coming toward them. Several reptilians were making steady progress along the corridor. Some of the prisoners raised their heads sharply on hearing muffled voices.

The gatekeeper stood in front of their cell, glaring angrily. Ligwa opened the door and burst inside with Morl. Tensing their muscles, the Crystallites stared at the huge guards towering over them, not knowing what was coming next.

"Move out, now! Before we eat you!" bellowed Lorc, while Ligwa and Morl scowled at the prisoners. With knees trembling, they stood up and obediently moved toward the door, not wanting to cause any trouble. They shuffled past each giant, feeling like pathetic insects. The unpredictable beasts grinned dangerously, threatening to stomp on them at any moment.

A cold sweat broke out along Aragonite's forehead and neck. He held his wife's hand tightly, making sure they weren't separated. Escalating pain exploded like dynamite in the center of Galena's being; it took a supreme effort of will not to double over. Aragonite managed a weak smile, which his wife was barely able to return. They were both thankful to have seen their daughter again. This mutual encouragement gave them the necessary strength to hold themselves together as they entered the corridor. It was important to focus on avoiding the thick white globs of saliva that splattered the grimy metal floor, just inches from their bare feet. When Galena glanced up again, there was a spiteful glint in Ligwa's glassy eyes. He stared unblinkingly at the woman's grim face, peeled his lips back, and sneered.

The prisoners entered the tunnel that contained the conveyor belt. Deep in the heart of the *Zonosor*, flames from the torches continued to throw leaping shadows across the walls.

Peridot was hauled up into the air first and placed roughly on the belt. He screamed as he landed on his injured foot. Topaz wanted to comfort him, but he was out of her reach. Garnet was about to speak to her husband with telepathy but Hematite, standing in front of Bixbite, caught her attention. The old man seemed to be in a daze and was breathing in a very unusual manner. Even though each breath was shallow and steady, his limbs and expression seemed lifeless. Concerned, she sent the elder a message. To her relief, Hematite was fine and appeared to be very much aware of everything around him.

"You are very afraid, Garnet," he observed in a low voice. The elder's speech was unhurried, his eyes fixed on hers.

"I've never been more terrified in my life!" confessed Garnet. She held Emerald tight, with the toddler's head buried in her mother's shoulder.

"Hold on to Bloodstone's words of wisdom," the elder offered as encouragement.

Topaz was finally able to join Peridot on the belt. She wiped the sweat from her brow, as the heat was making her skin prickle and bead with moisture. Suffering from dehydration, she found it difficult to breathe. The woman became weaker and weaker.

"Are you all right, Topaz?" asked her concerned husband.

"No, I … I … I feel dizzy and faint," she sobbed.

"I'm so sorry, my dear, but I don't know how to help you. Please try to stay strong for me."

Through his pain and exhaustion, Peridot somehow found the strength to slowly drag his shackled arm around in an attempt to comfort her. While Topaz was admiring her husband's effort, the movement caught Ligwa's eye. The guard gave Peridot's back a swift wallop with a metal rod, causing him to plunge forward. Tiny silver sparks appeared in front of his eyes as he fell onto Bixbite.

As the conveyor belt jolted along, the prisoners watched it gently rise and fall, taking them back toward the area where they had first boarded the vessel.

Hearing strange, low grunts, Onyx felt an urge to take a brief look over his shoulder. What he glimpsed was enough to make him quickly regret this action. They were approaching the foundry. In horror, he saw some desperate workers closing in on the conveyor belt. He drew closer to his father, who understood what was going through the boy's mind.

"Yes, son. There are many here that want to eat us all. But don't worry; the guards have been ordered to protect us."

Despite these reassuring words, Onyx remained in a state of silent panic till they had left the foundry behind.

# 15

## *Arrival on Mars*

Commander Girmlot, as Obsidian's second-in-command, was given the responsibility of ensuring the complete fulfillment of his captain's desires. While the *Zonosor* hurtled toward Mars, he set about assiduously overseeing preparations for the coming invasion.

This would have been a phenomenal challenge for most, but crafty Girmlot knew he was up to it. Leaving the navigator, Lieutenant Commander Razil, in charge on the bridge, Girmlot went to brief his subordinate officers. He personally inspected the masses of trident drop pods, large and small, designed to wreak havoc in the first wave of the attack, and the powerful war wreckers that would follow once the *Zonosor* was stationary. These contained the artillery units and twenty to forty warrior reinforcements, intended to complete the conquest of the planet. If the mysterious, fabled Red Army did exist, he'd draw them out and annihilate them. His brilliant plan was foolproof, he thought, confident of another easy victory. On his way back up the ladder to the bridge, Girmlot smiled as he pictured himself handing Mars to Obsidian and then feasting at last on those miserable Crystallites.

"I trust everything is in place for a swift victory, Commander?" growled Obsidian, who had already returned to the bridge.

"Of course!" sneered Girmlot confidently. "We cannot fail!"

A short time later, a bloom of light expanded at an incomprehensible speed as the warship slowed abruptly. Its flat tip, pointed like a spear, descended stealthily toward the red globe. The *Zonosor* entered the planet's atmosphere with lethal grace, its gun-metal gray surface shimmering. Girmlot, aided by Razil, carefully maneuvered the craft into orbit. Activating an iridescent light probe, Obsidian and the other two officers studied images of the rocky surface appearing on the screens. Canyons, mesas, and volcanoes abounded. There were many meteor craters and dry lake beds, all covered in red dust except for the polar icecaps.

Although there was no sign of any inhabitants, Girmlot wasn't going to waste time. "Release the first unit of drop pods *now*!" he bellowed down to the lieutenant standing ready several levels below.

In response, a gigantic bud opened beneath the ship's underbelly with a grinding twist of its overlapping metallic petals. Obsidian leaned over to look way down from the bridge through to the lowest level of the ship, eager to catch the beginning of his next battle.

The warlord rubbed gnarly hands together with glee as he observed the descent of a long line of small drop pods, all equipped with assault cannons that could launch short-range warheads designed to clear the way. Next a unit of larger drop pods was made ready. Each carried from five to ten ferocious warriors in full armor, as well as small cannons. These pods disintegrated after landing, giving the invading reptiles the cover of dust clouds to confuse any ground defense. Obsidian grinned dangerously, impressed by the sight of his armored soldiers stepping into their pods.

The *Zonosor* passed over colossal volcanoes set beside prehistoric fissures that exposed rivers of molten lava below. It flew over an enormous canyon, the ridges beside it clustered into folds. All the time, a continuous stream of drop pods sailed out of the belly of the *Zonosor*, small pods alternating with large ones. After each completed orbit, the vessel's course was changed so that it continually passed over new territory, covering more and more of the planet's surface with troops.

The deafening noise from the lowest level reached all the way up to the bridge. Machinery bringing the constant chain of drop pods into the launch area clanged and banged. As the jets on the undersides of the pods kicked in, their noise was amplified, echoing up through the ship. Reptiles rushed across the walkways that stretched between the gigantic reactors, scrambling along enormous tubes that hung like traps inside a hellhole. The skywalk was a wide structure suspended inside the *Zonosor*'s huge lowest chamber, with enormous coolant pipes looming overhead like knots of metallic intestines.

Obsidian peered through an opening and scanned the terrain below for any sign of the enemy he planned to annihilate. A new day was dawning down on the planet's surface. Nothing moved. *Strange*, he mused.

"Captain!" Girmlot yelled above the racket. "We may be nearing the site of the mysterious new power source."

"Where?" Obsidian eagerly studied the images of Mars

on the largest electromagnetic screen. Girmlot zoomed in on a group of ancient mesas, which commanded a view of a vast plain with many volcanoes, apparently either dormant or extinct.

"This looks like a good possibility," came the hopeful reply. "It fits the description Aphrodite gave you."

"Then what on Hades are you waiting for, Commander? Are you stupid? Stop the *Zonosor* right now and lower the ramp. Quickly! And start getting the war wreckers out immediately," the captain ordered.

"Do we really need the war wreckers, Captain? There doesn't seem to be any sign of resistance." Girmlot was confident that their undefeated legion was already victorious.

"Don't be a fool!" replied Obsidian scornfully. "We can't take any risks. If this is the site of the power source, there is sure to be some kind of guard. And if we are to defeat any form of opposition, we must attack strongly and destroy them immediately. Your objective will be to engage in battle with the main force of Mars's army."

The commander muttered something unflattering about the captain under his breath, then gave the necessary orders.

The noise level on the lower deck trebled in volume. Reddish-purple, forked tongues lashed out from between pointed teeth. Chaos seemed to reign as reptilians scrambled around, getting several hundred war wreckers ready to deploy. Girmlot had given orders for these gigantic armored vehicles to be loaded with ammunition ahead of time, but some of them had been missed. This added to the confusion. Boisterous mantras echoed throughout the ship as the demonic war wreckers began to leave the *Zonosor*.

Nevertheless, Obsidian, observing the action from a window on the bridge, was heartened by the sight of the immense barrage of vessels proceeding from his ship. He was confident that they would prove highly effective against the rumored Red Army, if it surfaced. The warlord was even vain enough to believe that if the weak god of Mars appeared, his war wreckers could easily defeat him too.

Once the first few squadrons of war wreckers were out, hundreds of automaton miners were released. They tore through the wastelands of Mars in pursuit of the mysterious new source of power. While there was still no sign of any resistance to the invasion, motley shadows gathered here and there in the harsh environment. Eerie reverberations were coming from somewhere unseen. Some sort of fog appeared, causing confusion among Obsidian's troops.

It was the Crystallites' turn to leave the spacecraft. They had been hauled up the long ramp in a cage. Now, still chained and shackled, they had to make their own way down, barefoot, under the watchful glare of the guards. Hematite, in the lead, hesitated for a moment and checked to see if the others were ready.

Ligwa gave him a shove. "Get a move on, you lot! I don't want to be squashed by a war wrecker, even if you do!" The guard narrowed his slitted eyes into a look so deadly and full of hatred, some of the youngsters felt their hearts pound and legs go weak.

Slowly and carefully, the disheveled prisoners in their dirty, ragged clothing made their way out of the *Zonosor* and down the metal ramp. Their first encounter with the sun on the surface of Mars was quite a shock for them, after living under the immensely thick cloud cover of Venus. The dazzling light blinded them initially, but their steel-gray eyes were able to adjust in a short time. Although the heat from the sun was greater too, their new olive-colored skin was able to withstand it without burning.

"Dad, what's that awful smell?" asked Onyx, wrinkling his nose as a sulfurous smell assaulted their nostrils. Countless cracks in the ground seemed to be the source of this strange, unpleasant gas. The older Crystallites suddenly became aware of the presence of an invisible force lingering nearby.

Garnet's eyes flitted from side to side as she examined the treacherous landscape. Nearby was a crater overflowing with thick, red mud that gurgled. Coils of steam snaked upward. In the ever-increasing heat, she remained silent, desperately clinging to the words spoken by Bloodstone's apparition.

Hematite looked up into the hazy pink sky, his distressed oval face framed by ice-white curls. Intense gray eyes filled with irrepressible tears that gushed down his soiled cheeks. He sobbed as blurred images tumbled through his desperate and fatigued mind.

Startled, the elder heard a deep, rumbling voice enter his mind. *"Hematite, you remember the prophetic words spoken by Bloodstone in the vision. The Rubatron, my invincible Red Army, will make contact when the time comes. Waste no time on sorrow. Collect yourself and rally your friends."*

The elder listened with gratitude as Ares outlined his plan. Garnet noticed the change in his face, and listened intently as Hematite proceeded to use telepathy to enlighten them all. Each one responded with a slight nod, acknowledging that the Rubatron's timing was everything.

As the elder shared this knowledge, the others felt revitalized. They began to look forward to this next chapter in their lives after the horrors of captivity. Mars itself was already giving them new experiences. It was so different to Venus.

Garnet responded with enthusiasm, "I can't wait to see the Red Army!"

Hematite smiled to himself.

# 16

## *God of War*

The Crystallites spent the day watching wave after wave of war wreckers and automaton miners leave the *Zonosor* and disappear into the treacherous red landscape. Still chained together, they were sitting on top of a small mesa nearby, as Obsidian had given orders for them to remain visible from the *Zonosor's* platform. Clambering up the steep, stony ground had been difficult, and they all had very sore feet. The guards, Ligwa and Morl, took turns basking and dozing in the sun.

From their vantage point, the Crystallites caught glimpses of vast halberds flashing and sweeping in the sunlight. Smoke and dust began to fill the air. As the day drew to a close, grotesque shadows drifted across the landscape. Nervous tension was increasing everywhere while Obsidian's troops waited for their enemy to appear. The nauseating stench of the sulfurous fumes rising from cavernous holes was relentless.

As the sun set, both moons were visible on the opposite horizon. An enormous fireball now appeared in the sky, blazing between the moons and pulsating rhythmically. Loud, rasping voices filled the air as the reptilians wondered how a colossal mass of orange flames could come out of nowhere.

Obsidian, dressed in his gleaming black armor, hurried out onto the platform. His eyes narrowed into a look of malice, and he gripped his sword tight. The warlord's body inflated.

On the bridge, Girmlot stared at the image of the fireball on his screen. It flattened out and hovered. He saw a face appear in it, surrounded by flames. *This must be a god*, the commander thought. With some trepidation, he realized this god was enraged, as the eyes were open wide and glaring vehemently.

Razil was trying to record what they were seeing on the screen. As he adjusted the camera, a hideous, discordant sound blared from the image, accompanied by violent flashes and crackling flames. The god had opened his mouth and roared. Razil flicked his tongue rapidly in frustration. Flames blazed out in several directions, causing the camera to jam. The screen went blank.

"What's going on?" bellowed Girmlot.

"Don't ask me! Looks like communication has ceased from whatever that was," said Razil. The pair stood in stunned silence.

From the platform, Obsidian glared at the face in the flames. The warlord reminded himself that the gods in this planetary system were weak. He had easily conquered the first two that he had encountered. This one would surely pose no real threat.

The flat, fiery face was beginning to be replaced by an enormous, three-dimensional male figure now materializing.

He appeared to be standing on a huge, sinister cloud that blocked half of the *Zonosor*'s right wing. The god's brazen armor was spectacular, from his enormous shoulder plates down to his greaves. A crimson velvet robe was swathed across his breastplate, which was set with a single, glowing, amber eye. He sported monstrous studded gauntlets and wielded a colossal shield and mighty sword. A white plume of horsehair cascaded from the top of his bronze helmet. A strange red mist outlined the god of war.

Obsidian stood his ground, snorting, panting, and howling obscene remarks. With a loathsome sneer tugging his mouth, he lowered his head slightly and scratched his scaly neck. The warlord glared at the god, noting his piercing black eyes, striking facial features, muscular physique, and undulant charcoal hair.

"Well, handsome, now who might you be?" sneered Obsidian, all emotion vanishing from his face.

"I am Ares, the god of war!" came the thunderous reply.

"Oh! Not another god! Don't waste my time throwing your meaningless name around; it doesn't impress me. I have already defeated two gods here, including Aphrodite, the supposed goddess of Venus! In case you're wondering, I left her for dead."

"Hold your filthy tongue in the presence of your betters," roared Ares, glaring at Obsidian. "Use Aphrodite's name in my presence again, and I'll kill you sooner rather than later." Ares's voice cut through the escalating tension as Obsidian turned away. "You place little value on the lives of your warriors, reptilian. And your belief in the invincibility of your army does not place you beyond my authority. I am the all-powerful god of war!" He tried to conceal the delight he was feeling at the thought of demolishing this ferocious army of reptiles.

Obsidian, in his ignorance, grinned dangerously. His tongue lashed out like a striking snake. Hot winds carried an ageless growl, raw and powerful, from Ares as he retracted into the fireball and left in a blur of speed.

Silently, a mass of invisible arachnids, the Rubatron, rose out of the ground, angry at the arrival of the Hadesians. They stood inches away from their foe, ghosting their every movement. Eerie whispers echoed all around the reptilians. Vague outlines of odd shapes drifted across the harsh backdrop, gradually filling the shadowy corners in every gorge. With an increasingly uncomfortable feeling, the invaders realized they were not alone.

The arachnids had eight strong black legs, each with six knees and ending in a sharp, armored point. They had an amazing ability to instantly increase and decrease in size, but mostly they stood only a couple of inches in height. Roux, their leader, was the exception, standing twice as tall as the others. Four white eyes, inset with black, vertical pupils, protruded from the tops of noseless faces. Their round, tough bodies were covered in thick scarlet fur, as soft as duckling feathers, but a fiery nature resided in their hearts. They could make themselves visible or invisible at will. Millions of years of volcanic activity on Mars had formed a gigantic network of lava tubes, the perfect dwelling place for the Red Army.

Countless invisible Rubatron now marched across the surface of Mars, their leader communicating orders using telepathy. Synchronized like an ocean tide, they went clicking and clacking, here, there, and everywhere across hardened lava. Many formed into lines on the horizon, while several hundred tumbled back down into the tubes. United in a common purpose, they waited for Ares's signal to set their world to rights.

Obsidian, still outside on the platform, heard a strange, barely audible clattering nearby, heralding the arrival of something primal and dreadful. Shadows began to swarm around him in the moonlight.

Ares came into view again, hovering near the rear of the *Zonosor*, his sword unsheathed. A magnificent weapon, it gleamed in the moonlight. He gave the Rubatron an unspoken order to set the Crystallites free. Oblivious, the warlord stood in uncertain silence while the clatters around him hissed into a chorus of whispers, coming from everywhere.

The Rubatron made contact with the prisoners telepathically. *"You are living in Obsidian's last hours. Follow our instructions carefully. We are the vehicle of light."*

Wondering what would happen next, the Crystallites struggled to their feet.

"What are you lot playing at?" growled Morl. Ligwa woke up with a start and glared at them. The Crystallites pretended not to notice. "I said, what are you playing at?" repeated Morl, loud enough to draw Obsidian's gaze in their direction.

The Crystallites' mesa was on a point of intersection of two ley lines, a place where the stonecutters, a unique group of Rubatron, could harness a powerful electrical charge. With it, they could open doorways, creating an interdimensional vehicle to transport them from one place to another.

In the lava tubes underneath the prisoners, these Rubatron swiftly wove networks of invisible thread by rotating fields of light—spirals of energy connected to those in tune with a higher vibration. The ground seemed to shudder as hundreds of small, unseen creatures leaped up onto the surface and wrapped the twenty-four surprised Crystallites in webs of invisibility. Others excreted an acid that melted the Crystallites' chains and shackles. The adults, openmouthed in amazement and wary of the guards, remained silent; the children tried hard not to giggle. Bizarre sensations stirred around their feet and went rushing up legs and torsos, down arms, and around necks. Without warning, the Rubatron pulled the threads tight. All disappeared from view without a trace.

Obsidian shrieked as his prized catch vanished right before his eyes. "Where are my prisoners?" he thundered in an earsplitting roar that echoed for miles.

Ligwa and Morl glared at one another in confusion. They became hyperactive at the sight of Commander Girmlot exiting the *Zonosor* and charging in their direction. A robust, gnarly hand grabbed each frightened guard. They fought hard to hold their ground as a vision of pure evil assailed them, demanding an immediate explanation.

Enraged, Obsidian turned to Ares, who responded by taking the form of a storm cloud. The god of war expressed his anger by producing a deafening thunderclap, unleashing his lust for blood. Ares sent a signal to the Rubatron to let them know he was about to declare war on the Hadesians.

Obsidian's body inflated again and he began panting, pacing the deck as he watched his enemy edge closer. The warlord was still confident, though, as he surveyed the enormous battlefield, well covered by his ferocious warriors who had never tasted defeat.

"Commander," he bellowed at Girmlot, who had rejoined Obsidian on the platform. "Let the fighting begin! It's going to be an easy victory!" A boisterous roar swelled from the restless troops below, keen for some real action.

The warlord leaned over the railing and acknowledged his senior officers; his beady eyes gleamed. The thrill of battle and the sensations of killing sent his body into a state of ecstasy. Obsidian's expectant warriors were tense as each squadron waited for the order that would send them once more into the fray.

# *17*

## *Battle*

On the *Zonosor*'s left flank, a blood red flag was raised against the darkened sky.

In response, Ares sent a signal to Roux. The Red Army's leader took a deep breath and then let out an incredible, ear-piercing sound that seemed to echo everywhere. Hundreds of thousands of bright red spiders began to emerge from the depths of Mars. As they marched, each one rose to seven feet in height, equivalent to their enemy.

All over the planet, the reptilians that had emerged from the drop pods were caught off guard. They spun round and round in surprise. As quick as lightning, individual Rubatron curled their front legs inward and then kicked out and up with all their might. Pointed feet caught the warriors beneath the jowls. Reptilian jaws locked with a click, and weapons were dropped as the victims hissed in extreme pain. The mysterious Red Army of Mars had begun a seemingly effortless slaughter of the invaders.

From the platform, Commander Girmlot bellowed orders to the junior officers. Hundreds more warriors poured forth from the *Zonosor*, wielding massive halberds. Huge blades keened through the air, but all missed their swiftly moving targets. The Rubatron lunged at the reptiles, forcing them to the ground in screeching fits, enough to burst their lungs. While armored warriors collapsed all around them, the spiders casually wiped their enemy's blood off their front legs and armored points.

The troops from the war wreckers were blasting in all directions with their gleaming titanium cannon. In the Hadesians' haste and confusion, they ended up hitting their own forces; the red flashes moved too quickly.

One squadron of ten war wreckers approached from behind an enormous geyser that bubbled furiously and spat boiling mud around the vehicles' metal legs. Several doors flew open simultaneously. Scores of warriors stepped out from the blue-lit interiors, their assault cannons already hunting for targets—too slowly, though. The movement of the strange scarlet beings was faster than anything they had seen before.

These reptilians succumbed to a swift, wicked assault, many falling into the geyser, screaming. Searing, needlelike legs of black, gouged reptilian armor off broad shoulders, severed limbs, and tossed bodies to one side. Warriors raised their swords in a vain attempt to shield their heads. Pointed legs leaped forward, slaughtering all within minutes.

Ares appeared on the battle scene and screamed in hilarity, delighted to be facing an enemy with some backbone. He brandished his sword and began to fight alongside the Red Army.

At the sight of the god of war engaging in battle, Girmlot ordered a large contingent of his finest warriors, splendid in their legion's colors, to confront Ares. They formed a line and opened fire. Bullets ricocheted off his blazing red mist and exploded as they hit the ground. Shells filled the air around him, bouncing off his shoulder plates and greaves.

This attack fueled the god of war's lust for blood. He charged at full speed through the hail of metal, his blazing fists bathed in lethal energies. Two dozen Hadesians were killed in one blow from his right arm.

Thousands more Rubatron rose from beneath the fiery terrain and joined in the mayhem, clattering all around and sending reptilians flying. The Hadesians crashed to the ground, groaning. The pain within them felt strange, as though it belonged to someone else. A treacherous voice entered their minds, speaking in an unknown language. The air was filled with smoke, fumes, and shards of debris. Obsidian finally stopped pacing and stared in disbelief.

A warrior attempted to strike the hilt of Ares's sword with a halberd. Ares responded by plunging the sword into the reptilian's face. As the wounded creature began to stagger toward him, Ares withdrew his sword and then shoved the blade through the Hadesian's stomach. Ares glanced up at Obsidian with a wicked grin as he felt his sword's energy field penetrate the beast's intestines. The god of war was reveling in the sensations of slaughter; he was enthused by the smell of blood and the stench of scorched flesh.

Girmlot and the captain, both hissing and panting, watched in anger and dismay as innumerable reptilians entered the realm of the dead. Obsidian's mighty warriors were defenseless against the unbelievable Red Army of Mars. The commander's face twisted in horror.

Warriors pushed their way into the center of a chaotic mass, where the Rubatron promptly swarmed over them. Claws screeched on metal armor like fingernails on a chalkboard. Blood continued to splatter and flow like red paint; it dripped off scaly skin and snaking tails. Too late, Girmlot, recalling an earlier conversation, realized that something horrendous and undetectable did in fact dwell within Mars.

Ares's grip tightened on his colossal sword. He let anger fuel his strength, determined to raise the score and humiliate Obsidian. Every missile the reptile forces fired was met by another fireball fashioned by the god himself. In a matter of hours, the warlord had lost over half his huge army and all his automaton miners. His drop pods and war wreckers seemed useless, and his extensive stockpiles of weapons and ammunition were vastly depleted, to no advantage. The total destruction caused by Ares and the Rubatron was astronomical.

In a single leap, Ares landed on the external deck of the *Zonosor*. Obsidian, caught off guard, took a step backward and tripped over his own tail. He scrambled to his feet and then ducked just in time as Ares's soaring fist swung past him. The warlord lashed out, slashing with his razor-sharp sword, but the thick plates of his enemy's armor turned the blade aside. Girmlot rushed inside to rally some officers to come out onto the platform to protect the captain, but Ares's swordplay neatly sliced their necks open. They were all killed without mercy while Obsidian, with Girmlot's assistance, slipped away back inside.

"You cannot run forever!" roared Ares after him.

With a treacherous smile, like a huntsman who had just outrun his prey, the god of war turned around and rejoined his Red Army on the battlefield. He set about smashing reptilian warriors with each swing of his sword and fist, fighting his way through the chaos. The Hadesians' swords had reaped a bloody tally in times past, and now the reptilians suffered the same fate as their previous enemies.

The captain had fled to his private chamber. He muttered, "Where is that Elderflower Elixir? I must hurry and drink it now to become immortal and defeat Ares!"

Razil, who had followed him, burst into the room and came to an abrupt halt. "We should leave Mars at once!" advised the lieutenant commander.

Obsidian twisted around. Reluctant to admit defeat, he screamed in frustration. Razil stood to attention. He knew better than to show any form of disrespect at a time like this.

With the precious decanter now in his grasp, the captain ripped the lid off and gulped down the entire contents. Moments later, he collapsed on the floor but was able to reach up and grab the corner of a table. Drawing on his last reserves of energy, Obsidian managed to pull himself upright. He bellowed at Razil, "Tell my commander to deploy every last war wrecker and muster all remaining troops. Arm them with every available weapon and send them out to attack those hideous red creatures. We will fight a war that Ares will not forget!"

The lieutenant commander quickly found Girmlot and relayed the captain's orders. After carrying them out, the commander joined Obsidian in his quarters.

Razil now went out on the platform, alone. He surveyed the battlefield. *This incredible Red Army is infinite*, he thought. With an empty feeling inside, he knew that there would be no holding out against it. The end was drawing near.

As the lieutenant commander watched, an enormous mass of Rubatron formed an interlocking array, an immense wall. They moved forward as a single entity and began an assault on the *Zonosor* itself, continuously crashing into the battleship.

Razil raced back inside to warn the captain. As he ran, he needed to dodge huge chunks of metal that were falling from the ceiling. The officer just made it through the crumbling entrance to the main hallway as a pillar came crashing down. "A lucky escape!" he muttered.

Razil entered the captain's chamber and watched helplessly as a section of its ceiling fell on Girmlot, pinning him to the floor and filling the room with dust. Obsidian roared in anger at seeing his prized Gothic architecture collapsing around him. As the warlord turned his huge head away from the disturbing sight, blood began to seep out of his body. The elixir was taking effect.

A large Rubatron entered the captain's quarters. Razil raised his sword, ready to deliver a deadly blow. In a flash, one of the arachnid's long legs shot up and sliced through the lieutenant commander's armor, cutting his thick torso in two and leaving him gasping. Razil, his vision blurring, stared up at the mighty red arachnid as he realized he was dying.

The Rubatron finished off Girmlot, but he decided to leave Obsidian alive to suffer alone the severe, painful consequences of stealing Aphrodite's precious elixir.

Countless Rubatron scurried and scrambled along the *Zonosor*'s corridors. On a special mission, one group went searching for Aphrodite's surviving sacred animals. Using telepathy, they found their way down to the hold and heard terrified chirping in the distance. The rescue squad paused at the sound of heavy footsteps around a corner. They instantly increased in height and curled up their front legs, ready to strike if necessary.

The guards moved on. One Rubatron pressed his pointed

foot against an iron door and inched it open. He slipped through quickly, followed by the rest. They crept along in the direction of the chirping, their sharp feet making a faint clicking sound on the metal floor.

Turning a final corner, the team reached the fifth chamber. Pleased to discover the door was unlocked, the leader cautiously pushed it open, holding his breath. As several Rubatron peered into the dimly lit room, it took all their willpower not to rush in. They were horrified at the sight of so many animals and birds squashed into cages. The lead Rubatron reassured the creatures using telepathy. *"We're here to rescue you. We must all move quickly. Trust us."*

In the guards' room next door, Sliv, Slod, and Slig were roused by the sound of iron bars rattling. They burst into the chamber at full speed, wielding their metal rods. Reptilians faced off against Rubatron. The guards lunged forward, hissing and waving their batons, their black eyes bulging in fury. The Rubatron swiftly seized their enemy's weapons, bringing them down on the reptilians' skulls with a heavy wallop. The hapless guards went sprawling backward into one another and collapsed in a heap.

Several Rubatron fatally pierced Sliv, Slod, and Slig with their pointed feet. Then others hauled the enormous bodies out of the way, allowing access to the cages. The Rubatron opened the metal cages with ease. They worked quickly and efficiently, wrapping up each of Aphrodite's creatures with invisible webbing. Lifting them carefully, they began to carry all the animals off the *Zonosor* to safety.

"Wait! What about Bloodstone's body? We can't leave her here!" cried a turtledove.

Some of the Rubatron agreed they should take her. In one swift movement, Bloodstone's tiny frame was wrapped in invisible webbing, scooped off the hard floor by an extra large arachnid, and carried into the darkness of the corridor.

The air around Bloodstone shimmered in crimson, indigo, and green; the web surrounding her became fragrant with the perfume of roses. Bloodstone's energy field increased, and the fatal wound in the center of her chest was saturated with color.

Along the *Zonosor*'s darkened corridors strewn with debris stumbled the remnants of Obsidian's army, overpowered and confused. Previously, on the Hadesians' way to Mars, the suggestion of the existence of a powerful god and a mysterious red army had seemed unbelievable. Now, the reptilians' utter defeat was surreal. Those near Obsidian's chamber shuddered at the horrendous sound of the captain's final, aggressive, rasping breath.

As if awakened by the sounds of battle, and desiring to erase all signs of the horrors that had just unfolded, a volcano near the *Zonosor* rumbled and began to erupt. A ravenous spill of molten lava flowed across the devastation of the battlefield and beyond. It consumed anything and anyone who dared to block its path.

Fingers of red-hot liquid rock reached out toward the reptilians' spaceship. The heat caused a sequence of reactions to take place in the cell where the Crystallites had been held. The mysterious egg-shaped object stirred into life. A brilliant beam of intense energy, like a searchlight, shot up from the egg and melted all the metal above it, clearing a flight path through the vessel. The egg had been recording the whole sequence of events since the *Zonosor* had entered the solar system. Now it was about to launch itself on a journey back to Hades. It began to shine with an ever-increasing brilliance, and then, in a flash, it was gone.

# *18*

## *Sense of Triumph*

Dark ash clouds slowly rolled away as the eruption ceased. Both moons were visible again, shining brightly high above the horizon. Moon shadows crept along the rugged, rocky mesas, adding a mysterious quality to the landscape.

The Crystallites had watched in silence as the battle ended and magma buried those responsible for their torment. Painful, vivid memories were difficult to erase: Lorc's cold, crude sneer and the nasty way the guards had glared at them while thrashing their tails. The loss of Bloodstone had deeply wounded the hearts of the twenty-four survivors.

With their enemy vanquished, the Crystallites turned to their rescuers. These spiders had stayed with the prisoners after making them invisible to the Hadesians. Several cheerful Rubatron waved their legs, gesturing enthusiastically and pointing down to a blood red river. The Crystallites, eager to escape the battle area with all its reminders, formed a line behind Hematite and clambered down the side of their mesa. Several Rubatron were assigned to each Crystallite for personal protection and assistance. The newly released prisoners were still wearing their amazing webs of invisibility in case a stray reptilian warrior was lurking about. However, the threads were so incredibly elastic that the Crystallites' progress was not hindered by them.

After walking along the river's edge for a while, their Rubatron guides halted at the foot of a huge mesa. Some of them extended spindly legs to signal that everyone must stop, while others indicated the need for silence. Using telepathy, they informed the Crystallites that the group should now leave the river and take a narrow path up the hillside.

Without hesitation, the twenty-four Crystallites set off again, faithfully following their unusual new friends up the steep, winding track. They wondered what the future held for them in this strange land. Assisted by the bright moonlight and their Rubatron protectors, they managed to climb over huge boulders with ease.

Finally, the leading spiders came to a stop on a broad ledge, hundreds of feet up, overlooking the hostile and desolate Martian landscape. By now, the Crystallites were feeling rather worn out. The effects of their horrendous ordeal were beginning to catch up on them after the strenuous climb. Some lay down on the hard ground while others explored their new surroundings.

"Come over here, everyone! This looks like a cave!" Garnet exclaimed in excitement. "Maybe we can sleep here tonight!"

"Yes, please! I do need to sleep!" moaned Galena. The emotional trauma of losing her daughter had taken a huge toll on her.

"I know, my dear," replied Aragonite gently. "We'd better get Hematite to check with the Rubatron first, though." While her husband went to look for the elder, most of the others joined Galena and Garnet near the entrance to the small cave.

Aragonite soon found Hematite standing with Peridot and Bixbite at the edge of the cliff, their gazes held by the spectacular sight of Ares sweeping back and forth over the harsh terrain. The god of war's malicious scowl hardened as he continued to hunt for surviving reptilians. His cheek bore a wide, curved scar as though a blade had gouged out a piece of flesh. Peridot and Bixbite caught sight of an unspeakable glint in his eyes. Alarmed by the god's fierce demeanor, they hurriedly took a few steps backward, almost knocking Aragonite over.

Hematite grinned. With excitement in his voice, he uttered a few words of encouragement to the three men, who tentatively stepped forward. Together, they surveyed the volcanoes and canyons spread out before them. Mars appeared to be a place of violence and destruction far beyond their comprehension; the planet's history was a mystery to them. As the remnants of the *Zonosor* caught the elder's eye, a slight chill made him shudder.

Seemingly from out of nowhere, an unfamiliar, taller Rubatron greeted them from behind. Hematite crouched down and scooped him up, cradling the Rubatron gently in the palm of his hand. He called the rest of the Crystallites over. Some of the women broke down in tears when the leader of the Red Army began to speak. "Welcome, Crystallites. I am Roux, the leader of the Rubatron. I am here to take you to meet Ares. He has been waiting for you."

Hematite gasped and said, "You knew we were coming?"

"Yes. The god of war has followed Obsidian's movements since his arrival on Mercury. Ares waited impatiently for

Aphrodite to ask for help when the reptilian warlord reached Venus. It was all part of the gods' overall plan for the destiny of our solar system."

"Why?" Hematite fought against a feeling of exhaustion, somehow finding the strength to continue this important conversation.

"You Crystallites have a role to play. In their long lives, the gods know there are no coincidences. As well as the destiny of the solar system, each life has its own destiny. The important thing is to keep moving forward toward your destiny, and that, my dear Hematite, is a natural gift."

"You see the destiny of our planetary system?" inquired the elder.

"Indeed, and I think you see it too."

"And Obsidian, was he part of this destiny?"

"Call it justice. He needed to pay for his horrendous war crimes. By falling for the story about a new discovery on Mars, Obsidian gave Ares the perfect opportunity to avenge the Hadesians' victims. The reptilian warriors were tough. I'll grant them that. They may have been strong too, but they were clumsy in their combat style."

"You sound rather disappointed when you talk about the warriors."

"Well, of course. I speak for my comrades. Jabbing our armored legs through scaly reptilian skins—how can we possibly improve our fighting skills when we're faced with such deplorable opponents? Anyway, we had some satisfaction in defeating them. Those arrogant fools wreaked havoc on Mercury and Venus."

"Roux, I cannot seem to find the right words to express how we feel. We are so very, very grateful to Ares and the Red Army for saving our lives!"

"The Rubatron always walk without question. We don't fear and we don't rest. This is why it was our duty to honor and protect Aphrodite's remaining Crystallites by carrying out a successful rescue. The gods and goddesses of our universe recognize that it has changed forever. And now, my friend, please place me on the ground again. I think it is time we helped you all out of your webs!"

The Rubatron scurried around, removing the threads from each Crystallite with a quick sweeping motion. Finally freed from all constraints, as one, the Crystallites raised their arms high above their heads. Vibrant rainbow colors poured from open hands. Rapid bursts of energies pulsated around their bodies in a sequence of rigorous rings, which spiraled up and glowed against the darkness. The display somehow communicated an atmosphere of deep respect and compassion. The watching Rubatron were delighted.

With wonder and even more delight, the hosts realized that their guests' appearance had changed. Their locks of flowing, ice-white curls again framed piercing blue eyes, and olive skin tones changed back to a beautiful pale bronze. Instead of dirty gray rags, they were clothed in dazzling white. Remembering their first sight of the Crystallites, the Rubatron congratulated themselves on such a victorious rescue.

Enthralled by their astounding beauty, Roux blinked in surprise, finding it exhilarating just being in their presence. The spider was filled with a great sense of awe at the sheer sight of such exceptional beings. Using telepathy, he asked Hematite to pick him up again.

Roux raised an extended front leg and touched Hematite's forehead, causing an electrical current, like pins and needles, to ripple through his body. The Red Army leader carried a powerful authority, emphasized by his deep scarlet color. Hematite felt a warmth flow from his heart across his chest and down each arm, simultaneously surging through his legs and into his feet. The elder felt amazingly alive.

The other Crystallites stood transfixed, watching in silence. Then they embraced each other. It was an extremely emotional time—delight tinged with sadness.

Finally, Jade let out a long, tired yawn, her arms and legs trembling from exhaustion. In response, Roux spontaneously leaped out of Hematite's hand. "Come and rest your weary bodies, my friends! There is some suitable accommodation not far away."

Roux led the way, giving the Crystallites a brief history of his ancient land as they went. After a short time they saw bright colors gathering near the entrance to a cavern.

Hematite and Bixbite peered inside, curious about the dim light on the far wall. Roux led them toward it, where they found some stone steps leading to a gate. Jade wondered why she was trembling. Galena's heart pounded.

At last, when all twenty-four were through the gate, Roux led them down a long, gloomy passage. Some took great care not to tread on anything sharp; others admired the many pillars carved out of burgundy stone which shimmered strangely.

Jade heard muffled voices coming from behind the wall. To their surprise, upon turning a corner, they were inside a kind of secret retreat. Their guide explained that they were in a dwelling built many centuries ago by Athena, Ares's sister.

Almost the entire floor was covered with what appeared to be an enormous red rug. Roux signaled for them to sit. As the Crystallites obeyed, relieved to get some rest at last, they realized they were sitting on masses of Rubatron. The creatures had somehow banded together to form the most comfortable bed imaginable.

Yet another surprise was in store for the visitors. As they began to relax, their host handed each one a glass made from cut rubies and already filled with elderflower nectar. The liquid's sweet taste brought back many happy memories. Noses were tickled by the elderflower aroma, evocative of springtime wanders through Aphrodite's gardens.

Filled with a sense of triumph, in due course they fell asleep.

# 19

## *The Symbol of Peace*

t daybreak, as the sky turned a hazy pink, the Crystallites woke up, revitalized. They were wide-eyed with delight to see a dozen or more cheerful Rubatron come scampering up, brightly colored flowers held firmly in their mouths. The spiders somehow knew that their guests ate flowers just like they did. The Crystallites had the ability to go without food for quite some time, but this meal was most welcome. It seemed like a lifetime since their last meal on Venus. Mothers smiled contentedly, watching youngsters devour their breakfast.

"Where did these flowers come from, Hematite?" inquired Jade.

"It seems like a miracle, doesn't it?" Hematite smiled.

The Rubatron who had formed the rug ate hungrily too, and then raced outside in a flash when Roux called to them.

Their appetites satisfied, the Crystallites bounded out of the cave, blinking in the sunlight and feeling rather jovial. They were rewarded with distant views of majestic mountains, in many shades of red, glowing in the early morning sun. Far away, one was erupting, belching forth spectacular columns of molten rock and massive ash clouds.

Roux called them over to his side. "Ares has sent a message. The time has come. You must follow me down the hillside to a clearing."

"Roux, I have a question, please. Do other life-forms within our solar system know of your existence?" Onyx asked.

"Yes, they have a little knowledge, but some are afraid of our Red Army and Ares's fierce temper. The god of war wants the inhabitants of each planet to know that there is someone who will fight for them in the event of an attack on their homes. There is also a place where they can seek refuge while Ares takes back for them what is rightfully theirs. Some are stubborn, though, and they do not ask him for help."

"How long will we be Ares's guests?" Peridot inquired.

"All will be revealed in good time, my friend. Let us prepare to resume our journey."

Hematite had been following the conversation. It helped the elder to keep his mind from thinking too far ahead and to concentrate instead on what was happening around him. With assistance from the Rubatron, he trusted their progress would be trouble free.

A fine drift of volcanic dust rose in the air as they began the next leg of their journey, walking in single file: first Hematite, with Roux perched on his shoulder; then Peridot with his family; followed by Bixbite with his. Aragonite and Galena were next, still feeling the loss of their daughter. The remaining two families happily socialized with the nearest spiders as they followed on.

Roux led them down a narrow, rough track with

rock walls on both sides. The stony ground didn't seem to bother Onyx and Jade. They were happy to mutter between themselves as they walked. Garnet admired the bright crimson of the cliff face towering far above them. A spectacular sight, she thought.

Midmorning, shortly after they rounded a bend, the air became much hotter. Their path lay along the top of a narrow ridge, like a causeway, across a stream of molten lava. Hematite crossed first, a little nervously, followed by everyone else. Safe on the other side, he stepped away from the raging heat. As he did so, the elder looked into the distance and caught sight of movement through the haze. "Roux, did you see that, or was it my imagination playing tricks on me?"

"No, that enormous creature you saw was the Screech Bird. It is more than twenty feet in length from a long, bulging beak to the tip of an incredible tail. The colors of its feathers are amazing. The cobalt and burgundy wings are tipped with purple, enclosing the blue-black, scrawny body. It has an absurdly long neck and thick legs, with three toes on each of its clawed feet. When Mars is faced with a catastrophic event, believe me, a single crack from its tail produces an earsplitting thunderclap. It is better if this bird remains unheard and unseen."

Hematite responded with a cautious grin.

Everything around them began to darken as the sun disappeared behind a thick blanket of black smoke. The path zigzagged, taking them closer to the foot of the mountain in a region filled with volcanic rocks.

"It feels like something exciting is going to happen!" announced Bixbite.

"Yes, I feel it too!" replied Topaz eagerly.

The smoke cleared as they traveled farther along the twisting track. It reminded Onyx of a maze as they wound their way between walls of cooled lava. A vulgar stench of sulfur lingered in the air, and the muted sounds of gurgling mud met their ears.

Hematite rounded another corner and spotted a sandy clearing up ahead, beyond a small ridge covered in ash. Their trek was almost at an end.

The Crystallites were surprised to find huge numbers of Rubatron approaching the clearing from all directions, coming up from their labyrinth of underground lava tubes. Thousands of pointed feet on the hard rock made a surprisingly loud racket. Many of the visitors felt an air of uncertainty envelop them as a massive wave of scarlet slowly drifted back and forth like an ocean tide.

The elder gently brought Roux close to his face. "Please, Roux, can you explain to my friends what is happening?"

"Keep an eye on the sky," Roux replied enthusiastically.

Parents watched their children enter the sea of red, contentedly sitting on the sandy ground among the Rubatron, who gladly made room for them. Time passed. The day drew to a close; the heavens seemed tranquil to all those waiting below. Content with the peace of the moment, Hematite crouched down, humming a cheerful tune. Those nearby enjoyed the melody and its rhythmic beat. The pleasant jingle was a distraction from the hissing and groaning of active volcanoes.

Suddenly, Hematite stopped humming, quickly straightening up. His hands fell limply to his sides while he tried not to stumble on the uneven ground. Miles away in the twilight, red and orange flames blazed between two rising, silver moons. The fiercely churning, fiery vision penetrated the layers of smoke that encircled the ancient planet. A loud clap of thunder was heard, followed by a terrifying sound of galloping hooves. Frightened children huddled together beside a hairline fracture in the ground. All eyes watched and waited, somehow knowing this was why they had been gathered together.

Ignoring risk and oblivious of danger, Ares stood in his chariot, drawn by two superlative black Friesian stallions. As they galloped across the expanse, their rapid and thunderous movements thrilled him immensely. Muscular equine chests were soaked in sweat; hindquarters were filled with power. There was a definite, savage beat, dangerous and consistent. Ares stepped back and gripped the reins firmly, preparing for his steeds' enthusiastic display of supremacy as they approached the clearing.

All the Crystallites were on their feet now. The adults felt reassured by the confident strides of the horses as they touched down on the hard lava, continuing to gallop at great speed. Ares drew back on his reins until both animals slowed to a prancing step and then stopped. Their breaths were harsh and explosive. They stamped impatiently.

Younger Crystallites hid behind their stunned parents. Blue eyes slowly peeped out, but disappeared quickly when the two horses snorted in their direction. The children felt the hot breath on their skin and found the animals' dark, glossy eyes confrontational.

The god of war presented an imposing figure, just as he had when confronting Obsidian. Once again, he was surrounded by swirling red mist. For a few moments, all living creatures present fell silent in awe.

Then a loud, spontaneous greeting arose: click-clacking from Rubatron feet and cheering from the Crystallites. Ares leaned nonchalantly against the chariot's side and waited for the applause to die down.

"Thank you!" he bellowed in a thunderous tone. "Rubatron! Yesterday you showed Obsidian what it means to fight against my famous Red Army! You achieved much honor in the war, killing more of your foe and losing fewer of your own members. You demonstrated real dignity in how you conducted yourselves in battle. I know you resent the arrogance of usurped authority, and that you realize that there is always honor to be found in standing for a just cause and defending the vulnerable. Strength, precision, and determination were some of the qualities you showed on the battlefield.

"Children of Venus, welcome! I am Ares, the god of war. Crystallites, from this day on, you shall be known as the Crystals. I know who you are and how you have learned to stand in the background: waiting, watching, and always knowing. Even when your road is difficult, keep going. The hardest walk leads to the greatest destination, the toughest climb to the most spectacular view. Remember, you never walk alone. I invite you to reside on Mars for a season. Here, the spirit of nature will cleanse you and prepare you for a future encounter with the inhabitants of Earth.

"But first, I offer my condolences to Aragonite and Galena. May the road rise up to meet you. May the wind be always at your back. May we, the gods, hold Bloodstone's hands in the palms of our hands. I will shortly ask the women to prepare her body for burial. We will honor her with dignity.

"Afterward, the Rubatron will lead you to the Promised Land. It is an enchanted kingdom where, centuries ago, my sister Athena, the goddess of wisdom and architecture, built an underground kingdom. A sphere of golden light protects it. There, you and the Rubatron can live together in perfect harmony and safety. You will also be reunited with Aphrodite's sacred animals.

"However, I am giving you one very important rule. After you arrive in the Promised Land, you must not try to leave this realm. If you do, I cannot ensure your safety.

"Once the burial ceremony is over, you must follow Roux again. He will continue to act in my stead."

Ares cupped his hands and blew some red mist into them. The mist condensed into a rich red-purple liquid that effervesced against his flesh. He blew again; the liquid solidified. Ares rolled it like dough between his palms, creating a glowing indigo orb of energy. It began to spin in his hands. His deep voice boomed out over the assembly. "Hematite, esteemed elder of the Crystals, step forward! Receive this symbol of peace."

Hematite obeyed and held out his hands to receive the precious gift. He gasped when it started to shrink, but was relieved to find this was only so it could fit into his smaller hands. He flashed a smile at Ares and bowed low.

Roux signaled for several of the younger women to gather near a smooth, flat rock. A large Rubatron came forward slowly, carrying an open coffin. It held Bloodstone's body, still wrapped in the web that had made her invisible. This spider was the one who had carried her body off the *Zonosor*. Taking infinite care, he dissolved the web and delicately placed her cold body on the rock. With a respectful bow, he stepped aside.

Another Rubatron came forward carrying a decorative silver salver. On it was a small urn filled with palm wine, an ornate crystal carafe containing juniper oil, and a length of white cloth made from silken thread. After arranging these on the rock, he joined his companion.

The five women gently bathed Bloodstone's body in the palm wine, anointed her with oil, and draped the cloth around her. Now prepared for burial, the girl's body was carefully placed back into the coffin.

Her parents and friends approached in single file, to mourn and pay their respects. They resumed their positions as Hematite stepped forward to conduct the ceremony. The elder had been caressing the glowing orb. Now he tightened his grip as he felt a raw energy flowing through it. He faced the crowd.

The service began with prayers in an ancient language. Everyone present, Crystals and Rubatron, fell on bended knee and bowed their heads in silence.

"The secret of eternal life belongs to the gods." Hematite raised the glowing orb high above his head. "And this orb will remain with Bloodstone for all eternity."

Directly in front of him, Aragonite and Galena struggled to their feet, tears streaming down their cheeks. Aragonite took the symbol of peace gently from Hematite's hands and moved toward the coffin. Galena watched in silence as her husband, with shaking fingers, placed the orb on Bloodstone's chest. Galena's breath came in short, painful gasps. They stepped back as more prayers were said, asking for their daughter to rest in eternal peace. The coffin was sealed.

Since early morning, a group of Rubatron had been busy handcrafting a crimson marble stele bearing an inscription. Another group had been at work digging a grave in the sandy ground. It was Ares's order that Bloodstone's body be laid to rest on his sacred land and sealed forever.

On command, several Rubatron came forward and carried the coffin to the prepared grave. They carefully lowered it, burying Bloodstone deep within Mars's blistering sands. Others secured the stele in place, a memorial for all to see.

A sweet scent, a combination of cinnamon, myrrh, and honey, spread through the air as the Rubatron saluted. Striking colors of many hues flowed from the Crystals' aching hearts.

Roux glanced at Hematite, reading the heartfelt pain that streamed across the man's sad face. Mixed emotions stirred within the elder. He felt an ache at being parted from Bloodstone but also felt anticipation at the thought of a bright future, living alongside his new friends in an enchanted realm.

*** 

At dawn, Ares paid his respects at Bloodstone's grave and headed for his chariot. With a farewell nod to the Crystals, he climbed aboard, cracked the reins, and leaned forward.

The god of war uttered a thunderous command. His horses snorted in harsh, explosive bursts, rising up on their hindquarters. Lunging, both horses thrust forward. Ares cracked the reins again. Demonstrating their strength and skill, the stallions leaped into the air together, hauling Ares's chariot behind them. In seconds they were gone.

From below, all that could be seen was a flash streaming across the sky like a burst of lightning. The horses went galloping at full speed over vast stretches of the dangerous and unpredictable planet, then up between the sleeping moons and on their way to Venus.

# *20*

## *The Journey Continues*

"Can I go to sleep now, please? I'm so tired!" Jade yawned and looked up at her mother. After Ares's departure, some of the youngest Crystals felt exhausted.

"I think we could all do with a nap! Let's go see Hematite," replied Garnet.

An hour or so later, the sun was clear of the horizon. Roux came over and tapped Hematite on the shoulder. The elder roused himself and the others from their short but deep slumber.

"Come, Crystals. Let us start on our way. It is far too dangerous for you to stay here any longer. Whirlwinds are coming. We must make haste!" Roux announced. A huge cloud of ash was being scattered across the arid landscape as hot winds blew in from the south. Thick clouds of smoke were billowing in the west.

Roux scrambled back across the sandy ground and made a high-pitched sound, a single note. The sound was soft at first and then increased in volume until twenty-four Rubatron responded. The effect on them was instantaneous.

They jerked up like puppets. Their bodies filled out and their pointed legs grew longer and longer until the arachnids were each the size of a pony.

Bixbite took a deep breath, then said nervously, "I am not refusing, mind you, but I am not sure about riding a spider."

Peridot laughed. "Neither am I. But you must admit it does look like fun."

"It sure does," added Topaz, "and much less tiring than walking, too!" She came forward with confidence, eager to be the first to mount an arachnid.

"What about the little ones, Roux?" queried Garnet, worried about Emerald.

"They'll each have two or three other Rubatron holding them securely on their spider ponies," he replied reassuringly.

Satisfied, Garnet now gave Bixbite some encouragement. Clutching a handful of thick fur, he managed to be the next one to hop on a spider. Seated in a secure position, he was pleasantly surprised how comfortable it felt. Soon all twenty-four were on their Rubatron ponies, ready to go.

In one giant leap, Roux landed on top of Hematite's spider and waved a spindly front leg, indicating the way. The elder's body jolted as his Rubatron pony began to trot. There was a general feeling of excitement as they set off toward a new dwelling place in this strange, mysterious world.

The Crystals rode confidently along a sometimes treacherous path, chatting among themselves. A mass of red followed close behind, flowing around them like an ocean tide. The click-clacking of pointed, armored feet on hardened lava produced a regular rhythm. At times, Bixbite felt his Rubatron rise and fall, and he tightened his grip around thick fur. When his spider jumped, they soared high together, feeling alive and free. Moments later, they would land safely.

As midday approached, the travelers reached the foot of an ancient, volcanic mountain range. It had been eroded over time so that it resembled a series of plateaus. The heat became oppressive as they climbed. A current of wind brought some relief, but with it came a foul stench from the many active volcanoes erupting in the distance.

To Onyx, they presented a gloomy sight. The lava flows reminded him of gnarly, clawed hands, twisting in some sort of patronizing call. He couldn't stop thinking about Bloodstone, but he took comfort in remembering her message. While a full understanding of her sacrifice escaped him, he knew that what she had done on the *Zonosor* was somehow important and good.

On level ground atop a plateau, Onyx and Jade felt playful. They left their parents' sides and raced ahead to ride in front of Hematite and Roux on their spider ponies. Other children decided to join them. Hundreds of eyes were following them as they glanced around excitedly. The wind picked up, tossing long strands of Jade's hair across her face. She licked her lips and tasted the sharp tang of sulfur. The smell seemed to cling to her skin, stinging her nostrils.

At the far side of the range, they came to a stop at the edge of a steep cliff. The view was spectacular. Jagged peaks on the horizon looked like a line of monsters constantly exhaling, as columns of smoke rose from active volcanoes. Rising out of the plain below was a large caldera formed millennia ago. Inside this huge crater, the Crystals saw what looked like the ruins of an ancient city. At the foot of the cliff was a river of molten lava, spanned by a walled bridge made of stone.

The view from the top the cliff included other wonderful sights too. A bizarre-looking mountain jutted out of molten lava, almost as if the magma were eating away at the land it had formed. Above, a haze hung in the air like a sheer curtain, covering the highest point. Inside the haze, there was an incredible display of luminous colors, twisting round one another and blending with gray clouds.

Peridot moved his Rubatron closer to Topaz and placed a hand on his wife's arm. The shimmering light looked like nothing they had ever seen before. They were both captivated by the immense power the iridescent light generated. Feelings of optimism and peace flowed through them.

Topaz tilted her head back and said, "It sounds crazy, but this chaotic planet has somehow become our safe haven." She closed her eyes and quietly savored the moment.

A voice from behind them roused everyone from their musings. "Come on now. We must keep moving on our journey to the Promised Land. There isn't much time!" urged Roux.

He pointed out the way—back a little, where they could go carefully down a steep slope and into a canyon. All made it safely down. Then they followed the canyon through to the foot of the cliff, coming out near the bridge they had already seen from above. It was late afternoon by the time everyone had crossed the bridge and gathered safely on the other side of the red-hot river. The Crystals sighed with relief.

They traveled around the outside of the old caldera, Hematite chatting with Roux. "Do you think Ares will find our beloved Aphrodite?"

"I believe he will. Your goddess has been through a

tremendous ordeal. We never disturb the god of war unless our situation is life-threatening. We carry on by ourselves until he returns. When one season of life ends, another begins. Lay your struggles aside now, my friend. Remember, you have put your faith in much mightier hands."

A commotion caused Hematite and Roux to hurry to the fore, noting that the other Rubatron had stopped. In the fading daylight, their eyes beheld the large silhouette of a wounded reptilian warrior scrounging for food. Roux's demeanor changed as he raised an eye and clamped his mouth tight shut. Then he produced another high-pitched sound; this time it blared like a siren. The reptilian raised his snakelike head at the sound of the war cry.

It was the most terrifying sight the elder had seen since the recent battle. Hematite's eyes darted from the warrior back to Roux's face. He turned to the other Crystals and realized some of the women were crying. The children, who had been singing softly, were silent.

In response to a silent command from Roux, several arachnids grew to the height of their reptilian enemy. One more high sound came from Roux. Immediately, some of the tall Rubatron formed a barricade around the riders. Two others approached the Hadesian. His black, beady eyes glared at the Red Army warriors. He began to pant and his open mouth revealed rows of razor-sharp teeth and a forked tongue that flickered feverishly.

With a great hissing sound, the reptilian charged, his tail whipping violently from side to side. Lightning fast, one Rubatron struck him hard in the center of his chest. The blow sent the creature spinning and tumbling to the ground. Struggling to his feet, he winced in pain. The Hadesian dropped into a defensive posture and moved toward his rivals. Within seconds, he was struck again and fell onto all fours. He dragged himself off, yelling in pain. Another ear-piercing yell was heard a few minutes later in the distance; a fall into a hot geyser had apparently finished him off.

Roux apologized to the Crystals. He had been aware that some of the Red Army had let one wounded Hadesian remain alive, out of curiosity. However, Roux realized now that that had been a mistake. The creature posed a threat to the safety and well-being of his charges. The elder accepted the apology, and the whole group resumed their journey.

The two moons rose as evening fell. In a fog-locked landscape, the travelers continued through the night and on into the early morning hours, without disruption. Some of the Crystals managed to take short naps—not sleeping too deeply though, as they had to keep hold of their Rubatron ponies. Dark clouds hid the moons at times but dispersed at first light.

Just as dawn was breaking, a strange sight met the eyes of the Crystals. In the shadows, they could just make out a huge stone structure. They wondered why the Rubatron were forming into parallel lines in front of it. Looking around, they realized the whole landscape had changed dramatically from the day before.

There were no volcanoes here, just lots of small mesas, thickly crammed together. The ground was much lighter in color. Most surprisingly, there were shallow, carved trenches, like long, crooked fingers, with tendrils of water flowing in them. Dominating the scene were two enormous dark-grey sarsens. They were bonded together as if forming a gate. This seemed to be a sacred land where the sky and planet were shadowy and the sun was a distant blotch. Here and there, fog rose from tiny holes in the ground. A great, craggy peak raised its crest high above them, appearing like some form of silent protector.

As they edged a little closer, Roux leaped down to join his companions on the ground.

# 21

## *Almost There*

Through the curling fog, Roux let out another ear-piercing sound. The Rubatron's leader was sitting in front of the sarsens, his six legs folded in an unusual manner. Within a few seconds everyone felt a deep rumble in the ground. Roux smiled at a faint giggle from some of the younger Crystals.

With eyes closed, the leader breathed in softly through his tiny nostrils. Roux held his breath for a count of ten and then formed a small oval shape with his mouth. As he exhaled, his breath pierced a hole in the invasive fog. He was enjoying this moment. Excitement escalated inside him at the knowledge of what was about to happen. All preparations had been made. He felt invigorated as he waited.

Roux raised his head. His whole body was framed by a swirling red mist. It made the color of his fur a brighter red, and his black legs glowed. Speaking in an ancient language, with his eyed closed, he demanded, "Through the power of the gods, I order you to open!"

He opened his eyes, and those near him noticed they

were stark white with no pupils. His eyes slowly closed again, then blinked open. Now they were bright blue.

"Open now!" The sound was harsh and deep. Two voices rolled off the same tongue, the words marginally out of sync with each other. His eyes closed once more. When they opened, two were dazzling white and the other two brilliant blue.

Nearby, Peridot looked at Topaz, his eyebrows arched. "There are two distinct voices coming out of one mouth!" she whispered in amazement. The others were watching in stunned silence.

Two tiny antennas grew on Roux's head. The ground vibrated with a series of crunches that were felt throughout the region. Some of the glowing red haze surrounding him condensed, dripping like water onto his fur. His voice trailed off, and the air was touched by the scent of sage. Slowly, the two sarsens began to separate, cracking apart. The strong bond that had been holding them together crumbled, dissolving into a gritty powder. As the fog cleared and the smell of sage intensified, Roux brought his front legs up toward his face and blew gently. The dust from between the boulders flew high into the air.

Many Rubatron streamed forward, taking up positions around the opening. Roux unfolded his legs and stepped forward. A strong gust of wind blew his thick fur, and the red haze brightened. A flash of white light cut through the fog and the boulders slowly separated. As Roux peered through the brilliance, his eyes grew larger, reflecting the light.

"Follow me!" Roux commanded, pointing toward a rocky path becoming visible through the narrow opening. Onyx and Jade were the first Crystals to ride through. Next came the excited elder.

After everyone was through, Roux clapped his front legs together. A wall of haze, white hot, rose from the crusty ground between the sarsens. The intense heat somehow drew the giant boulders back to where they had been and sealed them together again.

The group passed through a wide area filled with foothills, but in the bright glare it was hard to see much of the scenery. The two youngsters, riding just ahead of Roux, chatted cheerfully. Vibrant, colorful rays shot upward from their heads. They laughed at a bunch of boulders which looked like they had tumbled together, making a funny slanted wall. With excitement, Jade noticed snow-capped mountains, visible at times far above them.

It was midmorning when the pair stumbled upon a strange object on the ground, sitting between two large rocks.

"Quick, Roux! Come here! We've found something!" Jade squealed in enthusiasm, approaching the object with her Rubatron.

Roux scurried up. He increased in size, took a deep breath, and blew hard. Sediment swirled up in the air, revealing an ancient orb. Its surface was covered in a mosaic of lapis lazuli and it sat on a square silver salver engraved with an intricate grapevine pattern. This dazzling blue orb represented wisdom and truth.

Roux ran four legs across it and then traced the outline of each leaf on the platter with a front pincer. Drops of his fiery spirit trickled out from the tip of his foot, gently pouring over the orb. He then withdrew, stepping backward.

The Crystals were curious and formed a circle with their Rubatron ponies, watching intently. "This planet is full of spiritual mysteries. I can feel it," Bixbite whispered.

"There are no mysteries—just unusual abilities," Roux replied in a friendly tone, dusting off his red fur. Bixbite nodded as he rubbed the back of his neck.

A scorching hot whirlwind whipped around the orb, rich with sulfur, dust, and small stones. Thin bands of blue light rotated around it, and the orb started to spin rapidly, rising into the air. As the orb rose, the ground beneath it opened up. The salver fell through the hole and the orb disappeared from view.

"Wow!" Onyx exclaimed, staring down into the opening. He glanced quickly at Roux. "Is this a good thing or a bad thing?"

"It's a good thing. And it's been a long time since so much power has been released in such a small space," Roux replied.

Surprisingly, they were at once aware of the delicate perfume of frangipani flowers, carried on a most welcome, cool breeze. The odor seemed ancient and delightful as it wafted over them, coming up out of the opening in the ground.

Breaking the silence, Roux shouted jubilantly, "We're almost there! Come, Crystals, your Promised Land awaits you, deep within Mars!"

Excitement reigned as all the riders slid off the backs of their Rubatron ponies and gathered around the opening. Peering down, they saw what looked like an extraordinary translucent sphere, so enormous that they could only see a fraction of it. A blaze of white light was visible, revealing the top of a long staircase. It was cut into the steep side of a mountain the color of burgundy, and spiraled round and round as it descended, with no end in sight.

The Red Army's leader announced proudly, "Athena

carved these stairs herself. They will take us down to your new home, an enchanted garden kingdom." The stunned Crystals were lost for words.

First, the leader sent a party of Rubatron to stand on the outside edge of the staircase as a safety precaution. Next, he invited the soon-to-be residents to begin their descent. Some parents were a little nervous and clutched their children's hands tightly, maybe more for their own benefit than that of their offspring.

Although the mountain was surrounded by shadows, Onyx and Jade felt no fear, only excitement. Clasping their hands behind their backs, they skipped down the stairs, keeping a lookout for movement in the shadows. As Jade fell into step beside him, Onyx ran his fingers over the smooth corrugations of the burgundy wall. They came away with sprinkles of gold glitter. Jade smiled in delight. Without hesitation she reached over and touched Onyx's hand. Her small fingers slid over the glitter, causing her heart to beat wildly. The boy shook his hand in the air in front of Jade, sending her into peals of laughter as she continued downward.

# 22

## *The Promised Land*

The huge, translucent sphere appeared brighter and more transparent as the Crystals descended. It was now possible to see inside the sphere. Halfway down, there was a large platform, a curved viewing area, and the excited travelers hurried over to the edge for a better look. The brightness was unlike anything they had ever seen before. Delight was evident in the excited glances they gave one another as they began to realize they were finally looking at the Promised Land.

Their new abode, still a long way off down below, appeared to be a world within a world, with its own sun providing light just like the sun they had become more familiar with on Mars. In the distance, a mosaic path leading to an ornate stone bridge caught their eyes. Faint rainbow colors glowed along the water's edge. As they watched, silvery, coiling, semitransparent wisps appeared on the surface of the water. Moments later, the mist grew thicker, rising high in the air before dispersing.

Roux observed the faces of the Crystals, smiling to

himself at their looks of surprise and joy. Then he gave the elder a nod, a silent command to continue following the Red Army leader down the remaining stairs. As they progressed downward, the perfume of primroses filled the air and their feet were surrounded by churning, pastel-colored waves. Roux felt exhilarated when he turned around and looked up at their faces again.

The descent continued past midday, with more and more of the garden kingdom gradually being revealed. It was an exquisite sight, with endless acres of gardens and rainforests. For the first time since leaving Venus, the Crystals heard the melodic sound of foliage blowing in the breeze. Their eyes filled with tears as they all felt a shift in their subconscious. In that very moment, they heard the invisible whispers of nature no one could ever forget, an encounter so profound that it could only be understood through experience.

At the foot of the stairway, there was a guardhouse beside a cobblestone path. A little farther on was an elaborately woven floral archway flanked by two white Romanesque columns. After the trials and tribulations of their capture and imprisonment, they stood at the threshold of a sacred, hidden world. It had been created many centuries ago, inside a gigantic bubble deep within Mars, especially for them at this moment in the spiral of time.

Roux faced them, smiling. They gazed in stunned silence at the enchanting beauty of their colorful new home. The yellow afternoon sun shone bright against a sapphire-blue sky, bathing the whole landscape, with its many shades of green, in pleasant warmth. Other Rubatron too gathered around to see the reaction of their friends. The arachnids were not disappointed. Broad smiles lit up the Crystal's cheery faces; youngsters laughed as they trailed behind hushed parents.

The smiles became even broader when the newcomers heard a chorus of chirping and the turbulent flap of wings. Their joy knew no bounds when they discovered that all of Aphrodite's surviving creatures from the *Zonosor* had been rescued and brought here by the Rubatron. All the Crystals began waving excitedly to the many bluebirds and turtledoves circling above.

Aragonite spoke to Roux on behalf of the Crystals. "Up till now, we have remained quiet, hiding among the shadows, saving our strength. We don't need to do that anymore. Bloodstone is at peace now; her final resting place is here with us on Mars. Our journey has ended with a spirit of hope."

"Welcome to your Promised Land, Crystals," Roux jubilantly announced. He waved his two front legs to usher twenty-four Crystals, wide-eyed and elated, through the colorful archway and into their new home.

At once, the children darted off in all directions, eager to explore their magical playground, followed closely by their scarlet companions. The adults just wanted to rest for a while and enjoy their new surroundings. Lush green grass provided the perfect spot to admire the picturesque landscape. Multihued, perfumed flowers bloomed amid a wide variety of herbs. Orchards of heavily laden fruit trees and luxuriant rainforests beckoned farther on. In the distance, majestic mountains disappeared into fluffy white clouds.

Wandering through a wood, Onyx whispered in Jade's ear, "Can you hear that?"

"It sounds like a waterfall," she replied excitedly.

The intrepid pair raced through the trees, with their faithful scarlet spiders close behind, and arrived at a stunning scene. A stream cascaded down a rocky hillside and spilled into a deep blue lake, edged by hundreds of pink crystal flowers. Giant-size water lilies floated on the surface, and colorful dragonflies flitted in and out of the large leaves.

"This is even better than our lakes on Venus!" exclaimed Jade. "And there are pink crystal flowers here too!"

Onyx was more interested in wondering if he could climb up onto the rocks and jump into the water.

As the end of the day approached, Roux used telepathy to direct the Rubatron to bring all the children back. "There will be plenty of time for resting and exploring tomorrow and every day after. But now I must take you to see your new houses. Most importantly, Ares has prepared a banquet for us. Our successful journey calls for a celebration!" announced Roux proudly.

He set off, leading the group through an apple orchard buzzing with the sound of contented, busy bees. Roux took them down the mosaic path and over the ornate bridge they had seen from the platform earlier in the day. Farther on, the path widened and the landscape opened out. A village came into view, encircled by a wide moat where goldfish could be seen swimming around. The water was crossed by a wooden bridge, where a pair of Rubatron stood guard.

Once over the bridge, they came to a collection of beautiful houses built of white stone, set behind low walls with elaborate gates. Many of the homes were decorated with intricate paintings or carvings; each structure was unique, exhibiting its own architectural design.

In the center of the village stood a big, circular building, a community hall. Its walls were sheeted in mirror tiles and decorated with attractive patterns picked out in rose quartz. The roof had a spire, topped with a large amethyst prism.

Rays from the late afternoon sun passed through the prism and bathed the village in a magical mauve light.

In front of the hall was a village green, the luxuriant grass living up to its name. Scattered around the whole area were bubbling water fountains, also made from white stone, with a grapevine pattern carved into them.

The new residents were dazzled by the sight, completely overwhelmed. They embraced each other and chattered in excitement. Relieved to see his companions so ecstatic over their new dwelling place, Roux found himself laughing, a novel experience for the Red Army leader.

He waved his front legs in the direction of the far side of the green, where a lavish spread was laid out on a soft white blanket. A decorative silken web was strung overhead to provide shade. Everyone gathered around the banquet of freshly picked bouquets of flowers and herbs, bowls of delicious fruits and large carafes filled with fragrant elderflower nectar. Before starting to eat, the Crystals expressed their thanks by clapping their hands and producing a magnificent surge of energy.

"You are an extraordinary person, Hematite," Roux commented while enjoying the meal.

"Not really. I am just unique," the elder replied, smiling. They both laughed.

When the feast was over, everyone bowed their heads. They thanked Ares and prayed that he would find Aphrodite alive. Afterward, laughter filled the air. Hematite began to hum his familiar tune. The Crystals soon lost themselves in the tranquility of their majestic abode.

# 23

## *Romance*

It was cold, dark, and deathly silent.

The god of war hovered above Venus in his chariot, his eyes transfixed. He could only stare in horror at the devastation wrought by the wretched torment of the Hadesians' attack. A damp blanket of clouds hung low over the rocky landscape, with its many treeless mountains. Debris drifted across the scene, carried on twirling winds that raised dust devils in their wake. Topsoil had been carried aloft. Eventually falling, it had covered ruined villages in thick layers of dust, respectfully burying the dead.

A tide of despair crashed over Ares. Reaching its peak, it then slowly diminished, taking with it countless pleasant memories of happy times on this planet. Indistinct echoes murmured almost inaudibly. Except for the twenty-four beings he had rescued, the Crystallites of Venus had all joined the Ancients, leaving him to haunt the wasteland of Aphrodite's lifeless world alone and forlorn.

Ares flicked the reins, whooping through the gloom and commanding his stallions to descend. As the mighty horses galloped, showing off their power, his crimson robe whipped up in the ensuing wind like a victorious battle flag.

Where should he land? He had once known Venus better than his own secretive planet. Every mineshaft and mountain, every road and village—none had been barred to him, not even Aphrodite's own sanctuary. But now he felt like a stranger, confronted by evil spirits. Desperately trying to push emotion aside, he directed his steeds to fly over the endless paths.

The horses sensed something magical. As one, they reared up, their front hooves pawing the air. Ink-black manes fanned out as they galloped, steamy breath coming in billows of white from their open mouths. They took Ares over a deep gorge, somehow knowing the goddess had sought refuge nearby.

As they emerged from the gorge, the god of war bellowed, "I know this place! It's Aphrodite's Crystal Lake!" The horses snorted violently, causing the chariot to hit the ground abruptly. It almost knocked the wind out of him. The stallions stood tall. Their gleaming black eyes, ringed with thick eyelashes, widened. Pawing the ground, they neighed jubilantly.

Ares stood still, his heart aching as he watched the light flicker across the surface of the lake. He thought he heard a splash. Without hesitation, he leaped from his chariot, taking long strides toward the shoreline. Out of the corner of his eye, he caught a glimpse of shimmering scales, but he could make no sense of what he had seen. In a state of confusion, he dropped to his knees at the water's edge. His eyes scanned the water—watching, waiting.

The horses softly approached their master, heads low, nostrils flared. As he twisted round, their hot breath spread over his handsome face. One horse gave him a sympathetic nicker and nudge. His eyes were unseeing; Ares was broken, mourning. He took a deep breath and exhaled. Then, rising to his feet, his deep voice thundered for miles.

"The scent from your flowers has gone, along with your sweet breath I once felt. I've always been with you, never far away. I was your morning sunrise and your evening sunset. I heard your children's laughter, playing hide-and-seek in your forests. The winter snow will still fall on Venus, and your crystal flowers shall bloom again one day. If you could only look around, you'd realize that I am your everything."

Ares heard a faint whisper, a tearful angelic voice, coming from the center of the lake. "From the moment of your arrival, I felt an intense energy drawing you to me. Your powers seem to have stayed strong, while mine have gradually weakened."

Ares leaped up. "My beloved! You're alive! I thought I had lost you forever!" His heart was pounding, almost bursting with joy.

Brilliant beams of light broke through darkened clouds, sending shards of scorching yellow and gold over the landscape. Bubbles appeared in the center of the lake, sending ripples toward him. Ares stepped into the cold water; the sand greedily consumed his feet. He saw a flash of something of great splendor, silently slipping past him, just beneath the surface.

Suddenly, Aphrodite twisted her slender body around and leaped out of the water. Shimmering fins flared as she rose into the air, her glistening scales reflecting the sunlight. With a soft splash she disappeared back into the water, swimming energetically away from the shoreline. The goddess felt alive again!

Ares stood entranced, watching Aphrodite. He was in awe of the beautiful, mystical fish-form darting back and forth in the sunlight. Without warning, bright iridescent colors rose from the lake's center. Ares gasped. Thousands of luminous rays of gold and red light ascended high in the air. The waters, effervescing, turned a deeper, darker blue.

In a vision of loveliness, Aphrodite arose from the water. A glowing arc appeared above her new headdress of pink crystal flowers. The shimmering scales melted away, bubbling in the magical heat. Her magnificent fins, now soft like fabric, wrapped tightly around her naked figure. Arms outstretched and toes just touching the water, Aphrodite swayed her hips and glided effortlessly toward Ares with the gently rolling wavelets. As she drew nearer, their eyes met. The mighty god of war was almost overcome by a tremendous surge of emotion.

A warm breeze blew around Ares as he waited, breathless, for his goddess to reach him. Miraculously, new turtledoves and bluebirds appeared overhead, chirping merrily as they circled. He scooped Aphrodite up in his strong arms. Turning her head to look at him at him, she smiled as he carried her to the pebbly shore. The goddess of love and beauty blushed as her brilliant, cerulean-blue eyes held his piercing black ones.

Ares set her down softly on the shore. Holding her face tenderly in his strong hands, he gently kissed her.

They stood in silence, clasped in a tight embrace and surrounded by a feeling of peace. Ares bowed his head and whispered in her ear, "You'll never feel alone again, my darling, but your thoughts are free to roam. Do not cry over the past, for it has gone. Do not be concerned about tomorrow, for it has not yet arrived. Be with me in the present, and together we'll rebuild your kingdom."

The goddess murmured in agreement, and noticed that her fins had transformed into a new silken gown of oranges and reds. She had new jewelry and sandals too, just like the old ones. Golden curls hung around her exquisite face again now her hair was dry.

Hearing the horses stamping nearby, Aphrodite turned her attention to them. There was a wildness about these handsome stallions, but they never frightened her. The goddess admired their majestic, flowing manes and the feathering on their lower legs. She liked the way it swished as their enormous hooves clomped.

"Will you set them free, please, dearest?" she asked.

Ares nodded and complied; the grateful creatures whinnied their thanks. After drinking at the edge of the lake, they trotted off to enjoy freedom from the weight of harnesses and chariot. The intelligent, powerful animals soon broke into a smooth, graceful canter.

Ares took Aphrodite's hand in his, and the two began to stroll along the shore. The melody of the birdsong was entrancing. Its rhythm soon became irresistible. Before long, they instinctively embraced again and began dancing. Their faces shone as they entered into a new beginning.

# 24

## *Obsession*

*Twelve years later*

Onyx and Jade, both teenagers now, were in the library's archive room, inside the community hall. Hearing friendly shouts, they dropped what they were reading and dashed outside. In the distance, the green grass had turned a bright cherry red.

"Rubatron!" exclaimed Jade, shrieking with delight. They raced to the bridge over the moat, along with the other teenagers, and waited, cheering loudly.

As Roux approached them, Onyx asked, "Where have you been? Tell us all about your wild adventures."

Two weeks ago, Roux and several hundred other members of the Red Army had left the Promised Land on military business. Before their departure, Onyx had accidentally eavesdropped on a conversation between Roux and Hematite. He heard them talking about a spacecraft from Earth that had been on Mars since before Obsidian's arrival, but it had somehow gone unnoticed by the invading army. This intrigued him, especially when he thought he heard Roux say that there were Crystals on Earth too, living among its inhabitants. Maybe he could send them a letter, he thought.

Roux and the elder had also talked about a certain map. It was a map of the sacred city underneath the ancient, ruined city they had passed on their way to the Promised Land. But Onyx had confused that current discussion with the earlier one, and thought that the map related to Earth.

After hearing all this, Onyx had gone to find Jade, already forming a plan in his head. He found his friend on the far side of the apple orchard, picking daffodils and daisies for Galena's flower stall.

"Jade!" he called out as he approached her. "I just overheard Roux telling Hematite about a spacecraft from Earth landing on Mars! I really want to see it! Maybe we could slip away for a while and go find it? No one will probably notice," he said hopefully.

"Are you crazy? That's the most ridiculous thing I've ever heard you say, Onyx!" snapped Jade. "You heard Ares's warning. The memory of his thunderous voice still scares me. Who knows what misfortune could befall us up there? Anyway, how do you plan to slip past the patrolling Rubatron without being caught? They have eyes everywhere. There's no way I'm going!" She swung her basket round, nearly losing half the flowers as she stomped off.

"Jade! Wait! I'm bored! I just want to have an adventure!" Onyx shrieked, trailing behind her.

A few minutes later, Jade turned round and saw the deep disappointment on his face. Leaving the enchanted kingdom was an enormous decision, and not one to make impulsively. She knew in her heart that the possibility of such a scheme succeeding was extremely slim. "I think you should go talk with your parents about something as important as this," she insisted. "They are approachable, aren't they?"

Onyx shrugged and said nothing, but deep inside, he thought he already knew the answer. Remaining silent, he tried hard to picture himself going with his father to see the earthly vessel, and felt a slight stirring of hope.

After walking back through the apple orchard, Onyx and Jade arrived at the village green. They paused to take a refreshing sip of water from a three-tiered fountain before delivering the blooms to Galena at her stall.

Jade noticed Peridot strolling along, chatting with Hematite. "Come on, Onyx. This is the perfect time to ask your father, while the elder is with him. Perhaps together they could persuade Topaz."

"No, think I might give it a miss. I've been thinking about what you said earlier, and you're right. Let's go home and say nothing about this," Onyx said.

"If it's any consolation, I think you've made the right decision," Jade replied, nodding.

"Yes, I know," the boy said, forcing a smile. They walked home in silence, immersed in their own thoughts.

Over the next few days, Onyx tried to put the idea of seeing the spaceship out of his mind, but it was impossible. He didn't mention it again to Jade, but he did eventually tell her about the map. She thought finding it might interest him enough that he wouldn't come up with any crazier ideas, so she agreed to help him.

They decided that the best place to start was the community hall. After their chores were done the next day, they met at the hall to begin their search.

"I think the library would be a good place to start," suggested Jade.

Slowly opening the huge door, they were daunted by the soundless room. Aragonite was sitting at a long, antique table made of stone, and covered in dusty old books that looked very important. As the pair approached him, Onyx cautiously tried to sound as if he was clearing his throat. Aragonite jumped almost two feet in the air.

"My goodness child, you startled me!" he said in a tense tone.

"Good afternoon, Aragonite," said Jade politely. "I was wondering if we might look through some books, please."

He opened his mouth to speak, but sneezed into his cupped hands before he could begin. "Well, I suppose that would be all right, as long as you don't make any noise. I'm very busy, you know."

"Yes, of course," answered Onyx. "We'll be very quiet."

The two had no idea where to begin. They looked around at the countless books stacked on shelves from floor to ceiling. Eventually, one started on the left-hand wall and the other on the right. They spent several hours reading the covers of a couple hundred books without finding any hopeful-looking titles.

When it was time to go, they arranged with Aragonite to return the next day after lunch. The pair spent several more fruitless afternoons in the library, before Jade had an idea: "Perhaps we should try the archives. Maybe the map is not in a book. It might just be a document."

The next day, when they arrived as usual, Jade spoke with Aragonite about it. He sighed and looked at the teenagers. His face was kind, but it was obvious to them that he wasn't the slightest bit interested in what they were searching for.

"I'm not entirely sure it will be in there, but you can have a look as long as you put everything back where you found it," said Aragonite eventually. "The archives are through that door." He pointed to a small door in a corner.

Onyx and Jade thanked him and opened the door. The small, windowless room smelled musty and was only dimly lit by some crystal flowers mounted on one wall. Shelves from floor to ceiling, like those in the library, lined two walls. However, instead of books, they held mountains of folders, journals, and odd bits of paper. The fourth wall was taken up by cupboards and the door.

Without wasting any time, the pair made for the cupboards. Doors flew open as they began searching through hundreds of documents. Onyx became impatient, and leaving Jade to continue this laborious work, he turned his attention to some folders on one of the shelves. He thought he might have found something interesting: an ancient page with a complex illustration of interlocking symbols.

He had been taking it over to the light to have a better look when he had heard the friendly shouts signaling the Rubatron's return. Now, Onyx and Jade were at the bridge, waiting excitedly to hear what Roux had to say.

"On the last night of our twelve-day tour of duty, we climbed up a high mesa and observed a primitive spacecraft from Earth. It has been here on Mars for quite some time, but I hadn't been interested in it until recently. I decided to take a look. I have never seen anything like it before: a noisy apparatus sitting on top of a small hill, collecting samples. It paid no attention to us, though."

Onyx cast a swift glance at Jade and blurted out, "Awesome! When can I see it? And I know about the map too."

"Never! You know Ares's rule! By the way, what map?"

Roux scowled, but then he recalled his earlier conversation with Hematite. "Oh, you mean the map of the sacred city where the Great Shaman lives? We passed near it on our way here. But no, you won't be going there either. The land is far too dangerous for you to cross."

Jade sighed with relief and hoped she didn't have to spend any more boring afternoons looking for a mysterious map. However, she couldn't get rid of a worried feeling deep in the pit of her stomach. The girl was still concerned about her friend's obsession.

Everyone spent a pleasant evening at a festival in the community hall. There was a banquet like the one celebrating their arrival in the Promised Land, with gallons of elderberry nectar. Afterward, some people told tales. Others debated the laws and spoke of many things. Roux entertained them with stories of some of his challenges, but he made no mention of the alien spacecraft.

The next morning, Jade, Sunstone and Emerald were enjoying a breakfast of delicious gardenia buds when Jade happened to look out the window. In the early morning mist, she caught sight of a male figure moving furtively toward the wooden bridge over the moat. Sunstone, following her sister's gaze, saw him too. She reached over and lightly touched Jade's arm, bringing her sister out of her thoughts.

"Look at that secretive figure! Who do think it could be?" inquired Sunstone.

"I think it's Onyx," replied Jade in a flat voice.

"Are you sure? I just saw him a little while ago, speaking with his friend Jasper."

"Trust me. I know." Jade was holding a long, slender rose stem in her hand. She had a sudden urge to throw it in the direction of Onyx.

# *25*

## *Marc II*

$\mathcal{O}$nyx had left the village well behind and reached the ornate stone bridge when, through telepathy, he heard Jade greet him. He paused for a few moments, waiting silently in the shadows.

While he kept an eye on a Rubatron patrol, he heard her tone change. *"Where are you going, Onyx? Your secret mission won't lead to anything good, you know. You'll be sorry!"* His friend sounded irritated but he decided to ignore her and continue on.

It was vitally important for him to reach this alien spacecraft. Last night, after the festival, Onyx had secretly written a letter to Earth's Crystals. The boy was convinced he must make every effort at once to get it into the vessel, even though he had not been able to find any map of Earth yet to get an address.

Scents from a thousand blossoms filled the early morning air as Onyx hurried over the stone bridge and along the twisting mosaic path. He tried to work out the best route to the spiral stairs, wondering if he could get there without being seen or if he would have to engage in idle chit-chat with the Rubatron. It was no good resisting his burning desire; there was no way he could stop himself from making every effort to contact the other Crystals. He could think of nothing else.

Onyx congratulated himself at arriving unseen, or so he thought, at the flowered archway. He bolted up the first half of the staircase and stopped at the viewing platform to catch his breath. Dismay grabbed him as he heard the scamper of pointed armored feet fast approaching.

The fugitive was now surrounded by a dozen or more Rubatron, their angry voices alarming him. Onyx jumped back, then stood still, instinctively putting his hands on his head. The Rubatron saw shock in his eyes and a guilty expression spreading across his thin face. "You're in forbidden territory, Onyx! Go home at once!" one of them ordered.

Onyx frowned, thrown by the forcefulness in their voices. He glared into many irate eyes, trying to think of an excuse, and then looked down uncomfortably. Studying his feet, he spoke tentatively. "I'm … I'm sorry, but you don't understand. I really, really need to see the spacecraft from Earth!"

The Rubatron felt their rage intensify. Fury glared from their eyes. They peered into the boy's eyes, hoping to read them. Onyx tried desperately to ignore their mounting anger. He glanced upward, nervously wondering if he could make it to the top.

"Choose your next move with utmost care—your life depends on it!" warned a Rubatron, stepping forward.

After fighting off an unexpected desire to go home, he began to feel angry. "I want to see that spacecraft! Is that too much to ask?" He sat down defiantly as his resentment rose.

"Onyx, there is one thing you must understand!" the Rubatron continued emphatically. "Your well-being is very much more important than a primitive spacecraft!"

The stubborn teenager shrugged, unconcerned. "I have not come all this way to turn back now!"

"What?" the arachnid shouted. The Red Army spider was shaking in disbelief. He watched Onyx rise to his feet, turn round, and sprint up the second half of the stairs. All the Rubatron, not knowing what else to do, followed him from a distance.

At midday, Onyx reached the top of the staircase. He was relieved to be able to find the path through the foothills where the ancient orb had opened the way all those years ago, but he was a bit concerned about getting through the sealed sarsen gateway.

When he reached these huge rocks, however, he noticed that one of the trenches, still flowing with water, actually went underneath the massive stones. Although the way was shallow, he thought he could just manage to slide under the sarsens. Success!

His first steps traversed easy territory, but that soon changed. The landscape became increasingly hostile and unfamiliar. Years ago, he'd been carried through it at night on his Rubatron pony. He had to find his own way this time.

Volcanoes appeared. Onyx had to leap over many fissures, and the smell of sulfur made him nauseated. Dark clouds gathered, piling up on one another like mountains of terror. Lightning flickered within them like a candle flame shivering in a draft. A cold wind blew, and when he heard the faint but distinct sound of a thunderclap, fear gripped him.

The storm intensified, coming closer, then turned

and disappeared. Onyx breathed a sigh of relief, but this feeling was short-lived. There was a rumble from a nearby volcano, signaling an imminent eruption. As the ground began shaking, the boy ran as fast as he could in the other direction. He jumped over a fissure, nearly missing his footing and falling in.

A few minutes later, a windstorm seemed to be brewing. The wind whined and whistled loudly. Debris flew around him in all directions. Small rocks went flying past his head, forcing him to the ground. Onyx stood up again and tried to fight the powerful winds, stumbling over another fissure and gasping for breath. Feeling exhausted, he knew needed rest in order to regain his strength.

The runaway looked around for somewhere to shelter. Finding a suitable spot inside a group of boulders, he lay down, relieved to rest his weary head on the ground. He closed his eyes for a few minutes and dozed lightly.

Finally, the wind eased, then dropped. The clouds thinned. Onyx sat up, alert again. After rubbing his eyes and clearing his ears, he stood. At that moment, he felt like turning back, but his pride prevented him.

The Screech Bird had become aware of Onyx's plight. It began circling high in the air above the boy and let out a fearful cry.

The escapee was oblivious to the fact that scores of patrolling Rubatron had been watching him all this time from a distance. Some approached him now, saying angrily, "You need to head for higher ground for safety. We have been tracking that spacecraft for some time, and it's heading this way."

The stubborn boy whined, refusing to budge. He heard a familiar voice, weaving a veil of fury over the landscape. Roux had arrived.

"Onyx! *Go home!* Your parents, Peridot and Topaz, have been notified of your disobedience. They are very worried. You must return to them at once!"

"I'm not leaving until I see that spacecraft!" he snapped. In his selfish determination to carry out his plan, Onyx hadn't stopped to consider the impact of his foolish actions on those closest to him, especially his parents and Jade. Glancing up, he watched the Screech Bird slowly descending. The boy turned and ran away.

It was midafternoon when he spotted the tracks. With mounting excitement, he followed them for an hour or so. Onyx was overjoyed to find the object of his search, sitting on the bottom of a crater ten feet deep. Grinning from ear to ear, he shrieked, "Wow! Look at that! It is incredible!"

The sight of the craft sent him into a trance. He was awestruck at its huge size. Narrow at the front, it had a long, cylindrical center section, while the rear was conical. The underside of the cylinder had opened in order to allow six all-terrain wheels to descend and several robotic arms to unfold. The top had opened so that solar panels could flip up and catch the sun's rays, saving fuel. In large black letters, the name *Marc II* was clearly visible.

"It's amazing!" Onyx screamed gleefully.

There was a thump followed by a loud hiss. He heard a thunderous clap as its engines powered up—sensors had detected his presence. A second bank of black-and-gray-striped solar panels flipped up, and then a third. Onyx watched in alarm as the vessel started to clamber up the steep slope toward him. All thoughts of the letter he was carrying disappeared from his consciousness.

Delight rapidly changed to fear. He turned around and ran.

The extra solar panels increased the engines' power and the vehicle picked up speed, bumping along. In one almighty leap, a large mass of watching Rubatron increased in size and dived onto the vehicle in a desperate but unsuccessful attempt to immobilize it.

The terrified boy barely noticed the warning signs of another windstorm, as he sought refuge from the craft behind an enormous boulder. He was a little encouraged at seeing Roux and several other spiders join him, knowing they would do their best to protect him.

In spite of his fear, Onyx couldn't resist the temptation to peep out cautiously. He could see lights flickering wildly and there was a rasping noise coming from inside the craft. Blurred streaks of gray smoke billowed out from underneath it. A large circular opening appeared on the top of the spacecraft. Out came an enormous, black, flexible hose, rising and swirling around. The sight was compelling.

Roux screamed, "Watch out, Onyx! Duck!" But the warning came too late.

As if in an uncontrollable rage, the whirling pipe lunged toward the truant. In a flash, it sucked Onyx up, along with a Rubatron. The boy let out a bloodcurdling scream as the black tube swallowed him. Pain. Darkness.

The wind whistled as the storm approached. Roux and the others knew that it was only a matter of minutes before the landscape would be torn apart. The Red Army leader was deeply disturbed, for the first time in his life, as the reality of the abduction sank in. He felt responsible to Ares as well as to the other Crystals for the loss of Onyx.

A surge of red scurried behind the *Marc II* as it changed course and descended into a canyon. Its sensors were recording wind speeds reaching dangerous levels, so its cameras sought out flat ground to prepare for takeoff. Hundreds of arachnids surrounded the craft, watching helplessly as its whirring motors brought it into a vertical position, retracted wheels, arms, hose, and solar panels, and secured all openings. Three new legs appeared, slowly coming out of the conical end and raising the body of the vessel off the ground.

Inside the dark, cramped capsule, Onyx was still stunned by his terrifying experience. His body felt as if it were on fire, especially his head. He tried moving to get more comfortable but screamed in pain. "What are we going to do now?" he screeched as the horror of what had happened finally hit him.

Onyx's squeals of torment increased the terror the tiny arachnid was feeling as he searched frantically for a way out. The Rubatron hoped against hope that the spacecraft would not be strong enough to withstand the gale-force winds, opening up an opportunity for them to escape.

As the storm approached the apex of its fury, Roux and the Red Army had to acknowledge that there was no hope of rescuing the two captives. So they disappeared underground, seeking shelter in the lava tubes.

On board the spacecraft, a loud noise erupted, filling the prisoners' ears. The craft shuddered as the rockets fired up for blastoff. The captives felt the wind buffet the vessel as it lifted, then a feeling of weightlessness as they left Mars behind.

Onyx finally expressed remorse. "I'm sorry, Rubatron," he said to his small red companion. "My obsession has cost us a great deal."

The arachnid scrambled up onto the boy's chest but remained silent. Though the teenager couldn't see in the darkness, unlike the spider, he flinched as he felt the

Rubatron's gaze roam across his face. Crushed against the interior wall, he wanted to shrink away.

Finally, the brave Red Army soldier spoke. "Dealing with creatures from other planets within our solar system has never been an easy task. I fear we Rubetron have failed to meet Ares's expectations, and as a consequence, your life and mine are perhaps forfeit.

Onyx sobbed uncontrollably, his tears mixing with a gush of warm blood that trickled down his face. In spite of the pain, he tried to shake his head. "No, Rubatron. You haven't failed anyone. I have. All I wanted to do was send a letter to the Crystals on Earth, but now I've let everyone down, especially those who care most about me. Rubatron, my head hurts so bad!" Onyx closed his eyes and sobbed. Out of desperation he sent a telepathic message to Ares, hoping the planet's protector would rescue them. But the god of war was nowhere on the planet.

The boy could barely stay conscious. His Rubatron friend was very worried. "Onyx, talk to me. You must stay awake."

"How could I be so stupid, disobeying Ares?" Onyx murmured. He mumbled about how distraught his parents would be by now, knowing they might never see him again. His headache became unbearable. A feeling of calm swept over him as he drifted in and out of consciousness.

Slowly, the spark that once shone bright in Onyx's eyes faded. He struggled to breathe. The Rubatron watched him grow weaker. Blood continued to flow from the head wound as the boy deteriorated rapidly. A tormented howl of pain filled the prison capsule.

One hour later, Onyx died.

The Rubatron was left heartbroken.

He bowed his head in deep sorrow.

# 26

## Screech Bird

It had been midmorning that fateful day when Peridot and Topaz received an unforgettable visit from Roux.

"My friends," Roux began in a very serious tone, "I am very sorry to say that Onyx has broken the most important rule of this kingdom. He left our realm this morning. As a result, neither Ares nor any of the Rubatron, myself included, can ensure his safety.

"For some years now, a spacecraft from Earth has been exploring the surface of Mars. At present, it is in the area you passed through on your way here. When Onyx found out about this, he apparently formed a strong desire to find it. I fear he is now carrying out his crazy plan. I am about to set off with some Rubatron to look for him. Please stay here until I communicate with you again." The Red Army leader said good-bye and left.

The two parents looked at each other in horror and disbelief. They resisted the temptation to be angry with their son, realizing that there might have been some clues they missed, as to what was going on in his life. He had been spending less and less time with the other boys, and more and more time either on his own or with Jade.

"It's all coming back to me now!" cried Topaz. "I remember having a conversation with Jade several days ago. She mentioned our son was interested in finding some kind of map. Jasper also told me about Onyx talking to Roux about a map when he greeted him on the bridge. I thought about keeping a closer eye on him. When I spoke with Jade yesterday afternoon, she said that he had calmed down and put the worst of his crazy fascination behind him." She began sobbing.

"We need to stay positive, my dear," Peridot whispered, trying to raise his wife's spirits.

Topaz calmed down, blew her nose, and nodded in agreement. For the next few minutes or so, they attempted to use telepathy to contact their son. Despite their best efforts, neither one received a response.

Finding the suspense too hard to endure, the worried parents set off for the flowered arch to wait there for Roux to return. By the time they reached it, they were growing despondent again. Sunset was approaching when Roux and his companions finally arrived without Onyx.

Topaz felt her last meal start to rise up in her stomach, as though she was going to vomit. Peridot bent down and scooped Roux up, placing him in the palm of his hand. Roux extended one leg and stroked Peridot on the chin, looking deep into his sad eyes. Topaz leaned close until Roux's red features flickered into a blur as her eyes filled with tears.

"Listen to me very carefully, parents of Onyx," Roux said, breathing out warm steam with every word. "Onyx and one Rubatron have been abducted by the spacecraft from planet Earth."

Topaz and Peridot felt an icy chill go through them when they heard these fateful words. They shook uncontrollably and their mouths quivered. Struggling to speak, Peridot almost choked. He tried to catch his breath as his body went limp. The bereft father collapsed on his knees.

At the same time, Topaz looked frantically around the group. *Did I hear correctly? Abducted? Why would Earth take my son?* It did not make any sense.

Instinctively, she closed her eyes and used telepathy to contact Garnet. After breaking the shocking news to her friend, Topaz also collapsed in shock. Her husband squeezed her tight. Roux commanded two red soldiers to pick up the grieving parents and carry them home.

By nightfall, the other Crystals, who had gathered near the village green to wait for their friends, had heard the sad news. All hope of finding Onyx and the Rubatron alive had vanished along with the daylight. Everyone dragged themselves home to go to bed, but sleep eluded the grief-stricken parents. Lying on the sofa, exhausted, they finally began to doze lightly as morning dawned.

When the first few turtledoves began to cry, Garnet crept toward her friends' front door and eased it open, being careful not to startle them. To her surprise, Topaz and Peridot were on the sofa, wrapped in one another's arms, staring blankly. Garnet gave them each a kiss on the cheek, then slipped into the kitchen to make a pot of chamomile tea.

It wasn't long before Garnet heard the sounds of soft, pattering feet outside. She left the kitchen and greeted Galena and Aragonite at the front door. "Good morning. Thank you for coming," she said softly.

"We've brought breakfast. Topaz and Peridot need to

keep their strength up," Galena replied sympathetically, trying hard to contain her emotion. The memory of losing Bloodstone was still painful.

When Galena and Aragonite entered, they greeted Topaz and Peridot with telepathy. Topaz smiled weakly. Peridot simply nodded, then glanced around the room in a traumatized state. He appeared calm on the outside, as though he had layers of invisible armor curled around him, keeping his inner turmoil in check. Eventually, he managed to tell his friends that he and Topaz had been awake most of the night.

Just as Garnet was serving the chamomile tea in ornate cups, her husband and their three daughters arrived. Garnet gave Jade a hug as the girl's eyes flooded with tears. Jade cried inconsolably, the reality of her best friend's loss finally hitting her.

Saddened by the loss of Onyx, Hematite was making his way to the grieving parents' home when he happened to glance upward. A disturbing sight halted him in his tracks. The Screech Bird had entered the Promised Land and was circling high up. As the elder ran to the wooden bridge to get a better look, the bird glided away. His stomach churned as he recalled Roux's warning years ago about this creature. Hematite turned and hurried on his way.

Reaching Peridot and Topaz's home, he looked up again. In alarm, he saw that the Screech Bird was returning. The huge bird rose, cut left, and began to descend. Adjusting the angle of its body, it began gliding smoothly in slow spirals. The elder realized the creature was heading in his direction—the blistering red eyes were coming closer.

Hematite burst through the front door, shouting,

"Everybody! Hit the floor and cover your ears quickly! The Screech Bird is here, in our enchanted kingdom! It's about to crack its mighty tail!"

The others had no idea what he was talking about, but because he was their elder, they obeyed without question. Sunstone and Emerald clung to Garnet and buried their heads

Bixbite frantically wriggled along the floor to get close to Hematite. He noticed the elder was sweating profusely above his upper lip. "What's going on?" he whispered.

Hematite's face creased with concern. He just said, "Wait for it."

Peridot didn't move. Topaz stared through the window. Her hair stood on end when she saw a gigantic shadow drawing closer. It darted left, then right in a series of zigzags.

The Screech Bird spiraled down over the vast carpet of emerald green. It greeted the Crystals with a thrashing of wings followed by a single crack of its violent tail. The earsplitting sound, equivalent to the simultaneous cracking of a thousand whips, echoed for miles. Everyone in Peridot's house huddled together, shaking in fear and hoping they could survive another blow.

The monstrous creature took one last look below before allowing the wind to pull it higher. Flapping its giant wings, it disappeared, leaving the enchanted kingdom and returning to the gloom from which it had come.

Jade was the first to sit up. Others soon followed. The air was still, as if time were holding its breath. Looking into her father's face, Jade let out a weary sigh. Bixbite sat cross-legged beside her. He returned her gaze with an unspoken invitation. His daughter responded by moving closer and burying her head in his chest.

"Why didn't you tell me Onyx was heading toward the bridge?" Bixbite asked in a soft, patient tone.

Jade glanced up and tried hard to match her father's gaze. She struggled for a few moments with the enormity of his question before giving in. Finally, out tumbled all the words that had been trapped inside her since she saw Onyx leaving. Jade spoke about the library and how desperately her friend had wanted to leave the enchanted kingdom to find the spacecraft. The truth was, she blamed herself for what had happened to Onyx and detested her own foolishness. She wished with all her heart that something would swallow her up and save her from the heartache that was consuming her.

Slowly, Bixbite shook his head but spoke with kindness. He wasn't annoyed, but he was shocked. This father had never known any of his daughters to keep secrets before. For a few minutes, silence hung like a heavy weight in the room. The look that passed between Jade's parents did not go unnoticed.

At the unexpected gentleness of her father's words, all the hurt, irritation, and shame that Jade had bottled up inside now poured out with many tears. Garnet handed her daughter a white napkin and waited for the sobbing to pass.

Half an hour later, Jade was finally quiet. She sat quite still, her arms wrapped around her father's shoulders.

# 27

## *The Great Shaman*

$\mathcal{R}$oux arrived at Peridot's house with the usual troop of arachnids. "Good morning, everyone," he began in a serious tone. "Men, prepare to depart as soon as possible. We must seek out the Great Shaman in the sacred city. He is our only hope now. Although it means you must leave the Promised Land, I will be with you."

Peridot felt sick. He listened to Roux's voice as the Red Army leader outlined the plan, but his own thoughts were too overwhelming for him to comprehend what the leader was saying. His eyes shifted back and forth aimlessly. He hesitated at the thought of leaving the enchanted kingdom to search for some mysterious entity known as the Great Shaman.

Topaz was apprehensive. Aware that Roux's idea made sense, she struggled to come to terms with the thought of Peridot leaving her side to go on a long, possibly dangerous journey. Since Onyx's disappearance, Topaz had become reserved, as though the Rubatron were somehow responsible for her son's kidnapping. Something had changed inside her. Whenever she thought of the Rubatron, heat surged through her veins.

Clambering to her feet, Topaz rushed outside and dropped to her knees. Alone, the grieving mother watched the thick fog rolling along the horizon. Like a dark shadow, it seemed to consume the emerald-green grass of the foothills. The fog smothered the waterfall, causing it to weep. There was no one around to hear her frantic breathing, her silent cries of pain. Topaz felt lost and betrayed.

Sensing someone approaching, Topaz looked up. Although her vision was blurred, she recognized Roux. In silence, she stared at him, her whole body trembling. To her surprise, something kept their connection wide open. The compassion of a Rubatron was difficult to resist.

The grief-stricken woman's hair was bedraggled, her cheeks hollow, and her blue eyes ringed with exhaustion. None of that mattered to Roux. In a flash, he leaped into the palm of her hand and spoke words of comfort.

"Mother of Onyx, the pain of losing a child can never be described. You are hurt, sad, and broken. And you miss Onyx with all your heart, every moment of every day. May you receive the sincere embraces that we, the Rubatron, give you and your husband. This is our way of saying how much we care. May your tears be fewer as you feel the love and support of those surrounding you, despite your pain."

"I'm so sorry, Roux," Topaz replied, struggling with her emotions. "I know that what has happened isn't your fault. But why do you need to contact the Great Shaman and not Ares? Do you really think the Great Shaman will be able to help?"

"We must go to our sacred city first and seek counsel from the Great Shaman. He is the Rubatron's ruler from ancient times, our connection between the gods and the spirit world. Knowledge of this catastrophe will have already reached him, and nothing can reverse it. He will communicate with Ares. As a consequence, Zeus will cause Earth to suffer a terrible storm, beyond description. It will be a god-storm, the ultimate revenge for a crime committed against the Crystals. It is our way. Vengeance is always seen as an act of passion," Roux explained.

Peridot came outside and overheard the end of their conversation. For a moment he thought Roux was joking, but he knew better. Roux's tone was very serious. A chill spread across Peridot's back, his eyes widening. It took a second or two for him to realize that Roux was now speaking to him.

"Father of Onyx, we need to be on our way," Roux said, his voice firm. "Are you ready? We must leave for the sacred city without delay."

Hematite, Bixbite, and Aragonite came outside. Roux had convinced them that this was the best way to contact Ares.

The elder began to organize everyone, instructing them to meet Roux at the wooden bridge as soon as possible. Peridot raced back inside to pick up some items. After a quick squeeze of his wife's hand, he started off toward the bridge, his head held low, shoulders stooped.

Topaz had remained outside; her struggle with the grief of losing Onyx was far from over. Garnet called to her friend from the doorway, a sad smile pulling at her lips, but Topaz didn't hear. Distraught at her husband's departure, Topaz screamed, "Wait!" and raced after him.

Peridot turned and looked at her; he left the group and backtracked. As they faced each other, Topaz could see a different look in her husband's bloodshot eyes. He reached out and took hold of her trembling shoulders, gently but firmly. "The gods would not have brought us here if there wasn't a reason," he said patiently.

"What do you mean? Do you think they have put us here on purpose?"

"Yes! And Onyx has played his part in that purpose. There is nothing we can say or do to change the outcome for our son. I can only see death and devastation in our immediate future."

Roux was keen to get moving and called out to Peridot. He quickly kissed his wife on the cheek and whispered, "I shall return to you, my dear. Please don't worry. It seems my red companions are becoming restless." He let go of her shoulders and waved good-bye, forcing a weak smile.

Topaz cried as Peridot set off. Garnet called to her again, louder than before. A prickle of misery crept along the nape of Topaz's neck. She twisted round and stared blankly at her friend. A collage of horror invaded her mind.

Garnet, her daughters, and Galena stayed with Topaz for the rest of the day, offering their love and support in any way they could.

By midmorning, Roux's entourage reached the floral archway and the spiral staircase. More Rubatron appeared out of the shadows. All began the ascent in silence. Bixbite and Aragonite took the stairs at a run; Hematite and Peridot lagged behind. When Peridot began to struggle, Roux came back to help. With Roux and the elder either side of him, Peridot finally made it to the top.

In silence, they walked on through the foothills toward the sarsens. Roux was able to open this magical gateway again, and they went through, back onto the surface of Mars.

"After Obsidian's reign of terror," Peridot blurted, "I swore I would never walk this way again."

Hematite threw an arm around the shoulder of his distressed companion. "Unfortunately, my dear friend, life presents us with all kinds of experiences. And, as you know, they're not always pleasant ones."

Desperately trying to blink away black spots in his vision, Peridot strained his eyes. A wave of dizziness hit him, tipping him off balance. Hematite managed to break his fall.

Realizing Peridot was in trouble, Roux raised a leg and pointed to a Rubatron. The soldier instantly increased in size and scrambled over to Peridot. Peridot wrapped an arm over the arachnid's neck and pressed his head against the red chest. He could hear the Rubatron's heart beating. Every inch of his small body ached, but Peridot was determined to keep up with the others as they wove around the many small mesas.

Gradually, the landscape changed. Volcanoes appeared, and a thick fog descended. Roux called a halt and directed four Rubatron to become ponies. The four weary men were quite happy to ride instead of walking. At a signal from their leader, all the Rubatron blinked. Their pupils changed shape, enabling them to see through the fog. Now the group could keep making good progress through difficult terrain with low visibility.

They set off again, journeying toward the huge caldera where, twelve years ago, the Crystals had seen what looked like the ruins of an ancient city.

Arriving at the crater, Roux instructed the men to dismount. He led them along a path toward a rocky wall and then went on quickly, ahead of the group. At the end of the path, he stopped and cocked his head. Delicate nostrils flared as he breathed deeply. Alone, the leader stood still for a few moments.

Without warning, Roux crouched down, bunched his legs beneath his small frame, and leaped onto a dense network of silver webs that had appeared in front of him. Then he folded all eight legs over his chest and spoke a few words in an ancient language.

The rocks in front of him began to tremble. Moving apart, the boulders revealed a secret tunnel leading into the sacred city.

The men had paused after catching up to Roux. Some noticed there were odd-looking markings engraved in the rock wall above the leader. Hematite took a step forward, cautiously approaching Roux while he was scrambling out of the sticky mesh.

As if by magic, dim lights appeared on the tunnel wall. In the glow, they could see a rough track sloping downward. Not wanting to waste any more valuable time, in single file they followed Roux underground.

The tunnel twisted and turned, then unexpectedly narrowed. Peridot paused and leaned back against the rocky wall for a minute, inhaling deeply. Weary again, he was concentrating hard on keeping his footing on the uneven ground.

A strange feeling swept over them as they approached the end of the tunnel. Here they found a set of limestone stairs. As the four Crystals looked down, they saw a huge sphere, similar to the one containing the Promised Land. Inside this sphere was an enormous, maze-like city, built centuries ago. There were countless canals winding around limestone islands of differing shapes and sizes and covered in a variety of green plants. Cobblestone paths teemed with Rubatron.

The entire expanse was lit by a huge gold light, shining down like a sun. Hundreds of pillars blazed with a magical green radiance, reminiscent of glowworms. The pillars caused circles of light to appear on all solid surfaces, and the light from those in the distance merged into a single beam. As a result, the islands shone with an iridescent green light, and the rippling surface of the water shimmered.

Slowly descending the stairs, the visitors gasped at the beauty unfolding before their eyes. This sacred city presented a far more spectacular sight than anything in their enchanted kingdom.

"Welcome to our sacred city!" announced Roux as he led the way over ornate little limestone bridges to the largest island.

It was square in shape, and covered with rainbows of energy. In the center was a gleaming prism of light. Sitting peacefully inside it, on a huge green silk cushion, was an enormous mauve Rubatron. The visitors stood wide-eyed, gazing at the Great Shaman. His eyes were closed, and there was a powerful flow of energy that coiled around his body in threads of magenta and gold.

Suddenly, the Great Shaman opened his bulging eyes and asked Roux to step forward. The leader obeyed in silence and bowed. The shaman then ordered Peridot to approach. Peridot's face puckered. His heart pounded so strongly he thought it would stop beating at any moment, but he too obeyed.

In solemn tones, the Great Shaman spoke. "Father of Onyx, I am so sorry. It is my sad duty to reveal to you that Onyx has not survived the abduction. Although the

Rubatron snatched with Onyx has survived, we have lost him too, a precious member of our Red Army who willingly sacrificed himself. Thus we can say we share your unspeakable sorrow. Know this: families are united by love, and love fuels us. Its power is unfathomable. Open your mind to receive revelation.

"Throughout history, the name Onyx has been said to bring protection and to assist in the understanding of the wheel of birth and death. In time, your son will enable you to see that your separation from him is an illusion. He will aid the progression of life on Earth, and then there will be reunion. The people of Earth will experience something miraculous, bringing change to their world. I will send a message to Ares immediately."

The Great Shaman raised his head, looking up. Rainbow colors spun wildly around his body like a tornado. He let out a high-pitched wail that resonated through the sacred city and out across the universe.

# 28

## *Doors*

On Venus, an old tree stripped bare during the devastating invasion was beginning to show signs of regeneration. It seemed quite remarkable that it had any life left in it. Tall and strong, its trunk was reminiscent of an ancient warrior resting after a long journey.

The tree stood on a hill near Crystal Lake, where Ares was still spending time with Aphrodite, helping her to recover from her great trauma. In their walks around the lake, they often stopped to rest near this tree. There was something solid about it that attracted the goddess; she enjoyed being still and silent in its presence.

When they first noticed the new green shoots Aphrodite was delighted. She watched them grow into branches that were soon coated with clusters of delicate pink flowers. These filled the surrounding air with a perfume similar to jasmine, bringing back happy memories of her life before Obsidian's arrival.

The two gods needed to take care walking over the barren, rock-strewn landscape. The Hadesian miners had dug thousands of shafts, some of which were hard to see until it was too late. As they approached the tree, Aphrodite gasped in fright, feeling herself slipping down. Ares caught her just in time.

Before she could recover from the shock, an ear-piercing sound split the silence. The high-pitched wail came from all directions at once, making Aphrodite cover her ears, hunch over, and pull her head into her shoulders.

After the noise stopped, they looked up and were astounded at the sight of the old tree. Heavy droplets of water began pouring out of cracks in the trunk and along the boughs. The flowers were stripped off as the flow increased. Water gathered in an ever-increasing pool under the tree and then flowed down into the old mineshaft, taking the blooms with it.

Ares had recognized the wail. After a pause, he spoke. "That frightful sound was an urgent message sent from the Great Shaman on Mars." Looking up into the swirling gray clouds, he continued, "He's the only one I know who can raise that amount of water in a single note."

"Yes, I understood his message too. Poor Onyx! What shocking news! Sixteen is far too young to die." She sobbed at the thought of both her loss and that of his parents. "Why would Earth commit such an atrocious act against us? Right under our noses, too!"

"I must respond to the call and go back to Mars. I need to get my horses ready immediately," said Ares in an urgent voice. "One day, Earth will suffer for this outrageous crime!"

Aphrodite recovered her composure. "Perhaps, though, Onyx may bring peace to their world. I did think Onyx had a destiny to help Earthlings grow through a variety of experiences, both good and bad. But abduction of a boy and a Rubatron! I didn't think this was part of the universal plan.

"Yes, you must go back to Mars, Ares; the Great Shaman is waiting for you. Don't worry about me. I'll wait for you to return to Venus."

A flock of turtledoves standing near the water's edge took off. They circled for a few moments, then flew away. As she watched them, Aphrodite let out a long sigh before twisting round and locking eyes with Ares. "It breaks my heart to know that Topaz and Peridot are now left childless."

Ares's initial shock had subsided and was replaced by ferocity. The god of war bellowed, "This unspeakable event will stay with us forever! I will settle the score with Earth. I will see they are punished for their terrible crime. They have disobeyed the universal laws."

Ares enfolded Aphrodite in a loving farewell embrace. Aphrodite's heart thumped as he loosened his grip and whistled, calling the horses. She gripped Ares's hand and looked up at him, tears rolling down her pale cheeks. He kissed her gently and slipped his hand out of hers. She watched him march heavily across the rough ground toward his chariot.

The horses snorted and stamped, eager to set off. Ares adjusted their harnesses. Rearing and lunging in parallel, they thrust forward. In his anger, Ares cracked the reins harshly. There was an explosive burst of flames and red, fiery mist. The powerful creatures rose on their hindquarters and then soared high into the air, dragging the chariot behind them. The glowing scarlet mist swirled around Aphrodite in a sad, slow dance.

As the chariot became airborne, Ares looked down. There was a new, young pomegranate tree he hadn't noticed before. Its branches were covered in a mass of fiery red blossoms. Through telepathy, he heard the voice of his sister Athena: *"The fruit from this tree, and others like it, will ripen and produce more trees and fruit. They will grow at an astounding rate, bringing life back to thousands of acres of desolate land. This is the first step in the rebirth of the devastated Venus. In time, this planet will flourish again. I am also rebuilding the villages and causing the crystal flowers to return. Do not worry, Ares. I will take good care of Aphrodite while you are gone."*

Ares continued to look down as the horses rose higher. The flashes of fire around his chariot were reflected in the clear, mirrorlike waters of Crystal Lake. Soon the surface of Venus disappeared below its clouds. Finally, the planet was just a tiny speck in eternal space as his horses galloped on to Mars.

Near the lake's edge, a despondent Aphrodite surveyed the deserted landscape. Her long, golden hair hung limp over her forlorn face. She lifted one hand and smoothed it back, half wondering about wading into the cool water to become a fish again.

The goddess noticed some triangles of bright light leaping out of the gloom, as if doors had opened slightly. Narrowing her eyes, Aphrodite saw three actual doors appear in front of her, leading into the light. "Where did these come from?" she whispered in amazement.

Then, out of the corner of her eye, she saw Athena. "This your way out of Venus, Aphrodite, to find the healing you seek."

"But there are three doors here!" exclaimed Aphrodite.

"I know," replied Athena, laughing. "These are simply doors of destiny. You have to leave Venus through one of them."

"What's behind them, and what difference does it make which door I choose?" asked Aphrodite.

"Nobody knows what's behind them, but all subsequent events depend on which door you choose. Might I suggest the middle one?" replied Athena in a kind voice. "Let your heart choose and go!"

Aphrodite approached the doors carefully and stopped in front of the middle door. She paused for a moment, then bravely stepped inside, saying, "Good-bye, Athena. Thank you."

"You're welcome! Farewell, Aphrodite!"

Several hours later, Aphrodite woke up. She looked around, curious as to her whereabouts. Everything suggested that she had arrived in the gods' secret garden: fir trees, golden leaves, emerald-green grass, and a sapphire-blue sky above her head. By some miracle, she had been transported out of Venus and beyond the heavens.

The goddess lay on a soft carpet of fallen leaves. But what was that hard lump under her? Rolling over, she scraped away the leaves and uncovered an orb. As she grabbed hold of it, her heart almost leaped out of her chest. Cradling it in her palms, Aphrodite closed her eyes. "Bloodstone! Welcome home."

# 29

## *The Horn*

Ares spotted the old caldera above Mars's sacred city. With rage rising, he let out a thunderous roar and flicked the reins. "It is time to settle the score with Earth!"

As his chariot descended, the fierce god of war guided his black stallions toward two massive red sarsens. These resembled a pair of watchmen guarding the main entrance to the sacred city. The chariot hit the surface with a deafening sound. Ares pulled on the reins, slowing the steeds to a trot as they approached the opening. On the red horizon, the shoulders of the two rising moons were just visible.

The horses reached the entrance, eyes bulging and muscles rippling. As the horses trotted on the stony floor of the tunnel, their hooves sent up sparks that flickered in time to the thunderous beat. Now and then, the horses' flanks rubbed against the dimly lit walls, which were decorated with the pictorial history of the old city scratched into the rough surface.

Soon, stone walls gave way to shiny black marble studded with amethyst crystals. On either side were doors made from the finest oak trees. They had been crafted centuries ago by Athena, with massive silver hinges and elegant diamond handles. The tunnel came to an end at the foot of the same limestone stairs that Roux and his party had descended earlier.

A few minutes later, the god of war brought the stallions to a halt just behind the four Crystals, who were sitting comfortably on soft cushions. Ares's gaze fell on the Great Shaman. He leaped out of the chariot, bowed low, and then knelt in front of the huge mauve Rubatron.

Peridot had turned around to look at the horses, two huge black forms in the shadows. He panicked when they edged forward. As he felt their hot breath on the nape of his neck, his heart thumped wildly. He let out a sigh of relief as one stallion gently nuzzled the side of his small face, nickering softly.

Hearing movement behind him, Ares guessed his animals were becoming mischievous. Still kneeling, he twisted around and stared sternly at them. Both horses immediately stepped back, their hooves prancing. The proud creatures held their heads high and nickered, seeming pleased with themselves.

Ares leaped to his feet. He pulled Peridot up and grabbed him in a warm embrace. They stood in silence before the Great Shaman and listened as the giant arachnid spoke.

"Mars is about to declare war against planet Earth. Catastrophic consequences follow the crimes of abduction and murder. We will bring bleak days of despair and devastation to the people of Earth. The Rubatron who has survived the abduction will be renamed the Sacred Keeper. He will use his wisdom to evade evil. In time, he will become the guardian of the Crystals when some are born on Earth. Peridot, you and your companions must return to the enchanted kingdom at once. Son of Zeus, now is the time to seek assistance from your father!"

Ares turned and strode swiftly back to his chariot. A path of light appeared and transported all the visitors, including horses, to the side of the sphere. The Great Shaman reached for his bone-white conical horn, a larger version of the one Hematite had used on Venus to summon Aphrodite. One long blast of the horn reverberated throughout the sphere and beyond.

As the sound faded, the visitors saw the ground before them opening, and the enormous golden oaks behind the canals, spreading apart. They found themselves beside a deep valley, its floor hidden by a dense mist. In front of them, leading across the valley, was an ornate black marble bridge with tall, impressive columns along both sides.

On Roux's command, four Rubatron rose to the height of ponies. Ares stood in his chariot, waiting. When everyone was ready, the god of war cracked the reins. The horses' hindquarters trembled as they neighed and snorted angrily. The entourage, led by the stallions, made their way across the bridge.

Peridot was silent, struggling to understand the meaning of the Great Shaman's words. Reaching the other side of the valley, as if by magic, they were all back on the treacherous surface of Mars again.

For many hours, the horses and Rubatron ran at a furious pace across the harsh landscape. No one spoke; it was an awful day. Ares requested a brief break when he noticed the men were tiring, even though they were comfortably seated on their Rubatron. Then more furious galloping after passing through the sarsen gateway finally brought them all to the top of the spiral staircase.

The men dismounted and said their farewells to Ares, who let out a thunderous roar. Eyes widening, the horses stood high on their back legs and neighed triumphantly. When Ares cracked the reins, the mighty steeds kicked and jumped high into the air. Soon all that could be seen of them was a smudge of black, traveling across the heavens on an invisible path to Earth.

Garnet was waiting anxiously in her kitchen when she heard Jade shout, "They're back!" Garnet hurried to tell Topaz and found her friend slumped on the sofa. After relaying the welcome news, Garnet went into Topaz's kitchen to put the kettle on.

By the time the weary travelers reached Peridot's front gate, the aroma of freshly brewed peppermint tea was wafting through the open door. At that moment, Peridot received a telepathic message from Ares: *"Zeus, the god of lightning and thunder, has offered his assistance. Take care, my friend."*

Topaz ran outside to meet her husband with arms wide open; she embraced him, fearing the worst. The others went inside, leaving Peridot to give his wife the tragic news alone. Filled with deep regret, Peridot began to relay the message of the Great Shaman. Before he could tell her that Ares was on his way to Earth to seek revenge, her scream filled his ears, momentarily paralyzing him. Eventually, Topaz recovered enough for them to join the others inside the house.

A short time later, a bright flash lit up the front room. An intricately woven shroud of magenta and gold threads, with an apparition of Onyx inside its folds, appeared above his parents' heads. He was sitting in the crook of a golden oak tree, his legs dangling in the breeze and his head leaning against the old trunk. Silence reigned as a soft, angelic voice began to speak. "I never said I was leaving, and I didn't say good-bye. I was gone before you knew it. In life, I loved you dearly, and in death, I love you still. Deep in my heart, there is a place that only you two can fill. Please don't grieve for me; I am needed somewhere else. No one knows what the future holds, but in time, my past life will help future life progressions. Direct your thoughts toward me in times of mental and physical stress. Remember—I'll love you forever."

The apparition moved toward Jade, who said, "In tears I saw you sinking, and I watched you fade away. My heart was almost broken. You fought so hard to stay. Then I saw you sleeping so peacefully, free from pain. I won't wish you back to suffer that torment again."

***

Meanwhile, in the secret garden of the gods, Aphrodite heard the urgent call of the horn from beyond the heavens. The door suddenly appeared in front of her. She entered it and returned to Venus, arriving at the edge of Crystal Lake. Nervously biting her lip, she closed her eyes and tried to contact Ares with telepathy, waiting anxiously for some signal in response. The goddess whispered in an ancient tongue, "Where are you?"

At first it seemed her message hadn't reached him. Then a strong wind swept through the landscape, churning the waters of the lake and producing many dust devils on the shore. Aphrodite heard a distant hiss and the sound of reins cracking, followed by the beat of thunderous hooves. Two black stallions appeared as if jumping through a ring of fire. Ares's chariot made a slow circle above her. It descended further and halted, hovering above the lake's surface.

Ares spoke in an urgent voice. "I must leave the stallions here and set off for Earth at once. Zeus is a very impatient god. There is no time to waste, my beloved."

"Of course. Do what needs to be done. Leave them and go!"

Ares gave the reins a sharp snap. "Arrrrgh," he shouted and pulled the chariot round, making another wide circle before landing near Aphrodite with a loud thud. He leaped from the chariot and embraced the goddess. Whispering softly in her ear, the god of war made a promise: "When Earth has been dealt with, I will return to you."

Ares smiled tenderly at her as they broke apart. She raised her hands to stroke his strong face and then traced the line of his square cheekbones. Aphrodite bowed her head when Ares finally walked away. Within seconds, the god of war had taken the guise of a storm cloud.

A flock of turtledoves emerged from the surrounding treetops. With turbulent thrashing of wings, they soared upward, escorting Ares through the clouds as he began his journey to Earth.

# *30*

## *Settling the Score*

*B*ruce Prate looked up from his computer screen. The weather forecast for this Friday morning, March 19, 2021, was very favorable for the planned midair recovery of the *Marc II*'s capsule, but he still checked the sky for confirmation. Prate was the program director at the Moorata Space Center, located in a desert region in southern Arizona, fifty miles from Tucson. He enjoyed a spacious office with large windows on the top floor of the main building.

The center occupied an ex-World War II military aircraft testing facility, about twenty square miles in size, off Route 86. It sprawled across the dry, stony landscape. The top deck of the control tower provided supreme three hundred and sixty degree views all the way to the majestic mountains on the horizon. A new multistory building provided office space, while the older buildings contained laboratories, residential and recreational facilities, and storage for supplies and equipment. On one side of the complex was an array of white geodesic domes housing satellite antennas, and on the opposite side was a large fuel depot. Some distance away were hangars of different sizes. Adjacent to these were runways and a launch pad. There was only one gate, with a security checkpoint. From here, a single-lane road led up to the facility.

It was seven o'clock in the morning, and there was excitement in the air. The crews of several satellite trucks from the major networks, including APNB (Atlantic Pacific News Broadcasting), had arrived from Tucson, and were busy preparing for the historic occasion. Visitors fortunate enough to obtain passes were already arriving by coach, eager to witness such an event. After clearing security at the gate, they were driven to the outdoor viewing area. Many people who had missed out on passes were lining up in their cars on the edge of the road outside the security fence. The *Marc II* had been on Mars for the past twelve years, its encapsulated robotic probe collecting data and samples. This was the first of Earth's spacecraft to be equipped with the technology to return its capsule to Earth. Two helicopters were on standby for the recovery attempt.

Seated at his impressive desk, the director observed the hive of activity on the ground below, pleased he was not expected to interact with the crowd. He preferred to keep away from the public and the media.

Some scientists had annoyed him earlier in the week when they arrived at his office unannounced and wanted to debate the procedures to be implemented upon opening the capsule. They raised numerous concerns about the possibility of Martian samples containing microbes that might pose a threat to life on Earth. Impatient for his visitors to leave, Prate had politely assured them that great care in handling the specimens was indeed a top priority.

High above the Moorata Space Center, at 7:15 a.m.

local time, Ares tore through Earth's atmosphere and joined Zeus. The god of war greeted his father with a simple nod as he stepped out of the storm cloud.

"The humans on Earth have chosen the wrong path. They strive against the laws of nature. If the Sacred Keeper fails to complete his mission, their future will be catastrophic. And some of them are about to get a taste of my wrath right now! I am going to settle the score for what they have done to Onyx!" Zeus thundered and raised his golden staff.

Some of the people outside, eagerly awaiting the reentry, were scanning the sky for a sign of the capsule. Elvin Kriff, an APNB crew member, was one of the first to notice the arrival of two dark lenticular clouds high up, casting eerie black shadows. Sensing this could mean trouble, he immediately reported the sighting to his home base.

Without warning, around 7:20 a.m., there was a tremendous clap of thunder.

The director's tanned face turned pale at the unexpected thunder. His eyes narrowed when the radar screen showed the *Marc II*'s capsule coming down ahead of schedule. He desperately hoped its parachute wouldn't fail to open. He gave the order for the helicopters to take off immediately.

Just before seven thirty, there was an intense bolt of lightning. Prate glanced up quickly as both helicopters exploded simultaneously into balls of flame. Looking back at the radar screen, Prate found that the capsule had disappeared. He slumped back in his chair, his face ashen.

On the ground, the center staff were struggling to control the mayhem. Although the burning helicopter debris had fallen several hundred yards away, terrified visitors were screaming and running in all directions. The sky filled quickly with black, billowing clouds. Droplets of fire began to fall like rain, sparking multiple spot fires. Some of the visitors were scrambling back onto the coaches, pushing and shoving, while others tried to force their way into the buildings to take cover. The satellite trucks' crew members who were outside, rushed for the safety of their trucks. Outside the perimeter, many worried onlookers jumped into their vehicles and headed off at a reckless speed.

The deputy director, Brock Anderton, burst into Prate's office. "Sir! What in the world is happening? What are we going to do?"

Prate was jolted back to reality; he had half hoped it was a bad dream. "You tell me where the hell the *Marc II*'s capsule has gone! Has anyone given orders to the firefighters to get busy? I knew it was a bad idea to invite the public here!" he barked in reply, and picked up the internal phone to call the control tower.

In the control room, Alice Nichelle, the senior air traffic controller, took the call. She spoke hurriedly. "Sir, the capsule was caught up in a vortex, like a tornado. It seemed to be heading toward Colorado, but I'm sorry, sir, we have no idea where it has—" Her voice was drowned by an explosive clap of thunder. Seconds later, her voice returned. " …seems that several powerful thunderstorms are forming simultaneously, just off both the Pacific and Atlantic coasts! Meteorologists are perplexed. Wind speeds of over a hundred miles per hour are apparently possible, and many airports are already canceling flights. Massive rainfall is also expected, and flooding could begin in a matter of hours! Evacuations are already being planned—" The air traffic controller's voice was cut off by another thunderous roar. This time, it didn't come back.

Fierce winds now began to blow, and the thunder

claps became more frequent. Fiery rain was increasing too. Dozens of small fires were burning out of control.

Prate turned to Anderton. "You'd better go down and see that all the visitors get away safely. It won't look good if we lose anyone."

Anderton hurried off, but he had to take the stairs, since the elevators had stopped working. By the time he made it outside, he was relieved to see that the last coach was leaving, though it was dangerously overloaded. The driver looked terrified, especially when he could see nasty dust devils on both sides of the road ahead.

Above the melee, Zeus was enjoying himself. He swung his golden staff wildly above his head, unleashing his fury. He turned a lethal mixture of heat and powerful wind into a mighty column of fire. Grasping the staff tighter, the god of thunder swirled it faster until a whorl of fire formed.

By 7:40 a.m., the fiery column was thousands of feet high and moving across the open ground toward the buildings, leaving charred vegetation in its wake. Then, surprisingly, it changed direction and headed away.

The crowded coach headed down to the gate and out onto Route 86. The driver picked up speed, but his face paled when he saw a fierce-looking dust devil, full of debris, about to cross the road in front of him. He hit the brakes hard and swerved to avoid a piece of metal heading for the windscreen, realizing too late that he had overreacted. Passengers began screaming as the coach lurched sideways. It flipped over several times before bursting into flames and exploding. All aboard were killed instantly.

Back inside the perimeter, flashes of lightning continued to tear through the churning sky. The whorl of fire changed direction again, as if it had just been teasing by moving away.

An evacuation siren blared; dozens of personnel poured out of the buildings. They headed for the parking lot and jumped into vehicles. All the satellite trucks now hurriedly departed. Other personnel, including Prate and Anderton, decided to take shelter in the basement of their building.

The floor of the control tower's top deck trembled in the next few thunderclaps. One of the operators looked outside. His eyes widened and his jaw dropped open as he watched the whorl of fire approaching. He screamed, "Oh, crap! It's a finger of fire! I've never seen anything like it! Everybody get down!"

The huge spiral of flame reached the fuel depot and released a burst of energy like a blast from an atomic bomb. Blazing red and orange, it quickly escalated into a ferocious frenzy. Silence reigned in the control room before the entire tower exploded in a gargantuan fireball. More explosions followed till the whole complex was ablaze. The tremendous heat penetrated through to the basement of every building. Sadly, there were no survivors.

As if it had a life of its own, the blazing column headed toward the gate. Every single vehicle now attempting an escape was destroyed by fire.

By eight o'clock, the Moorata Space Center had ceased to exist. All that remained was a blackened wasteland. The inferno traveled across the open terrain for another hour or so, causing more terror and destruction before finally dying out as the rain started.

"Well, that was impressive!" Ares chortled in delight.

"My work here is done. The center has been destroyed, but the capsule is safe. The storms are on course to wreak more havoc. I have settled the score!" Zeus raised both arms. Dark clouds swirled around him, and in seconds he disappeared, leaving Ares to do the same.

# *31*

## *Response*

Agencies all across the country were frantically trying to work out what was going on at the Moorata Space Center. The media-wide blackout had resulted in the major networks dispatching backup crews from Tucson. An APNB van was the first to get underway, in response to Elvin's early warning. Its crew was led by Wilga Smythe, a senior reporter. Wilga was a tall, attractive, red-haired woman, who was accompanied by her producer, a camera person and a driver.

Several powerful thunderstorms had formed only that morning off the California coast; some had traveled swiftly eastward into Arizona. Torrential rain was causing flash flooding, making the van's journey take longer than expected. Meanwhile, Wilga was hearing reports about subsequent horrific events transpiring at the center, before all communications from it ceased. They sounded improbable: exploding helicopters, and clouds starting fires everywhere. The returning space capsule had apparently just vanished. There was an unconfirmed message from a ranch a few miles away about a huge "finger of fire." She urged the driver to go faster.

A mile before reaching the gate, they pulled over near the burned-out pile of twisted metal that had been a loaded coach not long ago. The sight of a partially burned human leg was something everyone wished they could unsee. After establishing that there were no signs of life, they continued on toward the gate.

Wilga hoped to enter the area to find out for herself what was happening. At the gate, an Arizona Highway Patrol vehicle was parked across the roadway, and the security building was a blackened pile of rubble.

In the pouring rain, Wilga grabbed an umbrella and stepped daintily down from the van. Smiling with her green, almond-shaped eyes, she introduced herself to Sergeant Gonzales while he remained seated in his vehicle, keeping dry. Using her most persuasive voice, she asked him for permission to drive on toward the center itself.

"Sorry, ma'am. I cannot allow you to proceed any farther," he replied, sounding officious. "It's way too dangerous. You'd best be gettin' yourself back into your van and headin' home. No point in stayin' here and gettin' wet." He didn't want the responsibility of looking after any reporters.

However, Ms. Smythe was not easily put off when she was on the trail of a good story. Wilga responded sweetly, "But Sergeant, this is major news! A possible terrorist attack even! Can't you at least tell me what you know? Please, Sergeant, I would really appreciate it," she added with a beguiling smile.

"All right, ma'am," he replied reluctantly. "I don't know much, mind you. Our vehicle and another one were only a few miles from the center when NASA lost all communication with it. We received orders to find out what was goin' on, and made it here just as the rain started. I sent the other vehicle on down the road to the center a while ago, but we've lost communication with it. I've radioed for backup, but risin' floodwaters are causing a delay. We figured we'd best stay put for now. That's about it."

"I think I may be able to offer you some assistance, Sergeant," replied Wilga cheerfully. "Our equipment includes a UAV, commonly known as a drone. Dougall can fly it over the area—with your permission of course—to see what's going on there. What do you think?"

"Why yes, ma'am. That sounds reasonable," he conceded, nodding his head.

Several minutes later, Wilga and the sergeant were seated in the back of the van, poring over the screen as the drone took off. Dougall flew it toward the center's buildings, following the roadway. Horrified, they stared at the vision presented to them. No life. Nothing. Nothing except a mangled, wet blackness.

With dismay, they discovered that the other highway patrol vehicle was upside down in a fast-flowing stream. They surmised that the driver had lost control in the torrential rain and skidded off the roadway. There was no sign of the two occupants.

Sergeant Gonzales bowed his head and crossed himself before exiting the van without speaking. He returned to his vehicle to send a report.

Wilga sat still in silence for a few minutes. She needed to get her emotions under control before filming a news bulletin for her boss.

As she stood in the relentless rain under a large umbrella, with the space center's charred security checkpoint in the background, Wilga Smythe looked calm and composed, her makeup and hair impeccable. No one except for her crew would have suspected the inner turmoil she was experiencing. The camera started rolling.

"This is Wilga Smythe reporting live outside the Moorata Space Centre, Arizona.

"Early this morning, crowds of eager spectators descended on the center, many with passes to enter the facility and watch the reentry of the *Marc II*'s capsule. It was returning from twelve years on Mars. Instead, they found themselves fleeing for their lives.

"It has been said that two strange clouds appeared in the skies above the center around seven fifteen local time, just minutes before the reentry was expected. Authorities have confirmed, however, that these were just two unusually dark lenticular clouds that completely disappeared after about an hour or so. A similar cloud was reported in Africa a few days ago. Local news media there, explained that the phenomenon was merely a mirage.

"Communication received from the space center this morning reported that the two helicopters, sent up to attempt the midair recovery of the capsule, somehow collided and burst into flames. The capsule was apparently caught up in a tornado. It has been declared missing, and the authorities are appealing for help. If anyone has any information concerning its whereabouts, please call the number now appearing on your screen. Proceed with extreme caution. Do not attempt to go anywhere near it. The capsule is considered hazardous, as its contents may be contaminated. Contact could be life-threatening.

"Reports indicate that burning debris from the helicopters falling from the sky looked like a long finger of fire. This seems to have caused the center's fuel tanks to ignite. The resulting explosion was so horrendous that all buildings were burned to the ground. Unfortunately, there were no survivors.

"Before the explosion, some visitors managed to flee the center. However, the last coach apparently met with an accident, and all on board lost their lives.

"Also this morning, powerful storms formed over the seas off both the East and West coasts. They moved swiftly toward land, with wind gusts of over one hundred miles an hour creating mayhem and ripping roofs off countless homes. Evacuations and rescues are taking place in some parts of the coast of California. Storms and erosion are eating cliffs away, taking million-dollar homes with them. For some people, it's a real-life cliffhanger.

"Torrential rain is causing massive flooding in states on both coasts. Mass evacuations are currently being carried out. Many airports have shut down, leaving over a million people stranded. There have been reports of several people being struck by lightning, some fatally.

"While the coastal states are being drenched, several inland states are experiencing high temperatures and strong wind gusts. This combination has resulted in the outbreak of many wildfires. The National Guard have been called out in some areas to assist the regular firefighters.

"Meteorologists are puzzled by these abnormal weather events occurring simultaneously right across the country. The death toll is climbing, and the property damage could run into billions of dollars. Questions are being asked—is all this just Mother Nature unleashing her fury, or is it something more sinister?

"There have been several reports from overseas of recent

unusual events. Waves up to fifteen feet high battered the south coast of Chile yesterday, with powerful storms wreaking havoc in this South American country.

"A recent news report from Europe said that in northern Spain, residents of the town of Astorna had a rude awakening in the middle of the night. The area was rocked by a 6.6 magnitude earthquake several miles away. However, seismologists said it was deep enough not to cause any significant damage. There were no fatalities, although residents reported that buildings shook for several minutes.

"This is Wilga Smythe from APNB reporting live at the Moorata Space Center, Arizona, where, as you can see, the rain is just not letting up. I repeat, the returning capsule from the *Marc II* spacecraft has been declared missing. If anyone has any information concerning its whereabouts, please notify the authorities by calling the number now appearing on your screen."

# 32

## *Awake*

Jett Stoen was increasingly worried about the dark sky in the east as he drove south on Route 319 in his beat-up Ford F-150. Accelerating hard over a bridge, he felt the tires grip the concrete. He liked the tightness of the steering wheel and the crisp roar from the warmed-up engine. Raindrops began to hit the windscreen. Freeway signs flashed past him, and fierce winds jolted his vehicle.

On his way to Deacon's house, Jett felt an impending sense of doom. With its dreary, churning clouds, the sky resembled a trough of freshly poured concrete. The drizzle soon turned into pelting rain, followed by loud claps of thunder. Jett watched the wipers clout away the water like an angry pair of hands.

Glimpsing a cluster of red lights up ahead, Jett dived for the brake pedal. Several vehicles had collided. More red lights flashed as a huge vehicle sped up behind him. Headlights were fast approaching—big, blinding lights. The ambulance thundered past, inches from his pickup, its siren wailing through the howl of the wind.

Jett sat in slow-moving traffic for about ten minutes. "I'm on three days' leave as of yesterday, and I've come home to this!" he blurted, feeling frustrated.

Deacon and Jett were now twenty-two, in their second year as second lieutenants. They were beginning to see how the world worked within the army, yet were still filled with the enthusiasm of youth.

The engine gave a low rumble as Jett weaved slowly through the traffic. He finally turned on the radio for a traffic report and caught the five o'clock news update. The news was alarming; catastrophic events were hitting in quick succession. "This is crazy! An explosion at the Moorata Space Center! Powerful storms on both sides of the continent! Abnormal weather conditions all across the country!" Jett exclaimed as he switched off the radio.

Finally arriving at the Rainers' home, Jett reversed up their driveway. He jumped out of his vehicle in the lashing wind and driving rain. There was a loud bang as the wind slammed the door shut, as though an unseen hand had hurled it in rage.

Within seconds, Jett was soaked to the skin. He raced up the porch steps, the wind ballooning his jacket away from his shoulders and threatening to pluck the keys from his pocket. Raising a clenched fist, he rapped on the door urgently. Then he cupped his hands on the glass panels and peered inside.

Hearing the knock, Lucy left the kitchen and hurried down the hallway, smiling when she saw Jett's face squashed up against the glass. She opened the door. Raindrops glistened on Jett's short, blonde, spiky hair. The corners of his mouth were turned up in a confident smile. Lucy looked into Jett's bright blue eyes, noticing his strong, straight nose.

His tanned face, with its wide, chiseled jawline, was smooth from a fresh shave.

"What are you doing without a raincoat?" she demanded. "Quick, get inside before you catch a cold. You might want to go upstairs and take a shower. I'm sure Deacon won't mind if you grab some of his clothes." Before Jett had a chance to ask where Deacon was, she had ushered him past the living room.

As they walked down the long hallway toward the staircase, Lucy said, "I was going to call you this morning, but Deacon mentioned that you wanted to spend some quality time with your parents. I really didn't want to disturb you."

Sensing Lucy's anxiety, Jett asked, "Is Deek all right?"

"He woke early this morning and decided to trim the branches around his old tree house. He hadn't made much progress when a bough splintered and fell, hitting him on the head and knocking him off the ladder. I dressed the wound and put some ice on his head, and then he went to sleep on the living room sofa. I'm getting a little worried. He should be awake by now—he's been asleep since just after nine o'clock. I've been checking on him regularly, though."

"I wouldn't worry too much, Mrs. Rainer. Deacon has a hard head. Maybe he's tired after our four weeks of maneuvers. We both know he can sleep through anything," Jett chortled.

Lucy nodded, reassured. "Well, you go ahead and get yourself dry."

"I'll wake lazybones up after my shower." Jett smiled.

"Oh, by the way, Deacon's grandfather is coming for dinner too. He's looking forward to hearing all about your adventures."

Jett raced up the stairs. Going into Deacon's bedroom, he turned on the light. The room was furnished in the same golden oak as the rest of the house. He rummaged around in several drawers of the tallboy until he found a T-shirt, jeans, and underwear, noting it was convenient that they were of similar height and build. After a short, hot shower, Jett stepped out of Deacon's bathroom and quickly dressed. He opened the wardrobe to look for something for his feet. At the back, half hidden, he caught sight of Deacon's old telescope and extraordinary binoculars.

As childhood memories flooded his mind, Jett turned and stared out the window. He recalled the time twelve years ago when Deacon was sure he had seen an alien spacecraft. The following day, the two of them had visited with Mrs. Mabbs. Over milk and chocolate cake, Deacon told them both all about it. Jett chuckled at the memory; it was a convincing story. He remembered, though, that this had been the start of Deacon's horrendous nightmares. Mrs. Rainer and Deacon's grandfather decided to put a stop to everything to do with astronomy for a while, including their planned visit to a research center. Deacon had been devastated when that trip was canceled.

Jett reminisced about sitting in the old tree house for hours while Deacon patiently pointed out the constellations to him. Aquarius, Pegasus, Orion … Deacon knew them all. Jett laughed quietly, knowing he was never really sure which one was which. "Well, my friend, there will be no stars tonight, just mayhem," he mumbled.

Becoming aware of an extraordinary coincidence, Jett was astounded. Deacon's sighting had happened around the time the *Marc II* had landed on Mars, and today was the very day its capsule was expected to return! He recalled the news bulletin. The capsule had gone missing that morning, and the Moorata Space Center, where it was to be recovered, had been destroyed!

Jett recovered his composure, found some shoes, and hurried back down to Mrs. Rainer, eager to wake Deacon and surprise him with the news.

Lucy and Jett approached the sleeping form on the sofa. It seemed a shame to disturb Deacon, but they agreed it was necessary. His mom shook her son gently, with no response. Then she tried again, a little more firmly. Deacon stirred slightly. After a couple of minutes, he opened his eyes.

At first, he just looked from one to the other, feeling confused. Strange, impossible scenes were flashing through his mind. Had he been dreaming? It all seemed so crazy, but at the same time, so real.

Jett was the first to speak. "Well, Deek. You certainly picked a good day to sleep through! It's only been the most eventful day this century! Horrendous storms on both sides of the country, wildfires inland, and a mysterious explosion at—"

"Stop! Stop!" yelled Deacon, suddenly sitting bolt upright and wincing in pain. "Don't say another word!" He looked up at them, his heart thumping. "If you were going to tell me about the Moorata Space Center in Arizona, I know it's been destroyed. They're all dead! And the capsule from Mars is missing!"

Jett opened his mouth, speechless. He turned to Lucy, "Mrs. Rainer, did you have the radio or TV news on at all today?"

Lucy looked bewildered and struggled to make sense of their conversation. She replied, "No, not at all. I was far too busy in the kitchen, fixing dinner and dessert."

The doorbell rang. Lucy jumped up, saying, "That'll be your grandfather, Deacon. I invited him for dinner too. I've already told him about your accident."

Deacon eagerly watched his grandfather approach.

"How's that bump, son?" Grandpa asked in a concerned voice.

Deacon reassured him. "I'm fine, thanks, Grandpa. How are you doing?"

"I'm fine, thanks, but I detect some tension in the air. Who's going to fill me in?" Grandpa asked.

Ignoring Grandpa's question for the moment, Deacon turned to Lucy. "How long till dinner, Mom?"

"Only a few minutes, dear," she replied.

"Thanks. I'm starving!" said Deacon. Looking around, he continued in a very serious tone, "I'm glad you're all here together. There's something I need to tell you. But first, no one is to say another word about today's events or switch on any news on the TV or radio. Can we please eat first? And then I will reveal everything."

# 33

## *Revelation*

No one really knew what to say over dinner. Everyone was preoccupied with their own thoughts. Deacon was the first to finish his meal; he broke the silence.

"What I'm about to say will seem preposterous. When I first woke up this afternoon, I doubted my own sanity. Almost immediately, I began to have flashbacks of a most unbelievable but realistic dream. Then, when Jett started talking about storms and an explosion, I knew that I wasn't going crazy.

"This morning, after Mom went to fetch some ice for my head, I had an unsettling experience—a vision of Dad. He looked so real. He gave me a detailed message about an alien warlord, Obsidian, breaking through a portal and attacking our solar system. Some inhabitants of Venus were kidnapped. Dad went on to say that I will have to find a red creature called the Sacred Keeper, and in time, Jett and I will have a special mission.

"After Mom put the ice on my head, I slipped into a dreamlike state, going back to Samson Hill, when I was ten years old." Deacon paused and looked at his grandfather. "In the dream, I heard your conversation with Mr. Allard and I saw what he sent to your computer. It was everything my high-tech binoculars recorded that eventful night, including Obsidian's warship. Mr. Allard said that we are living in times of deception, and that we can't rely on the government or the media to tell us the truth."

The colonel looked astonished but nodded in agreement.

For the next hour or so, Deacon continued to hold their attention by giving them a graphic summary of his living nightmare. He finished with a detailed description of the damage caused by the whorl of fire at the Moorata Space Center.

In the stunned silence that followed, Jett let out a slow whistle. "Now you've heard my version of today's events, let's see what APNB has to say." Everyone agreed.

They gathered in front of the television in the living room. Lucy picked up the remote control and found APNB's channel. They watched several items, not paying much attention, and then everyone sat up quickly when they heard the words, "In Arizona earlier today—". The report matched Deacon's story in essence, but Allard's warning was validated. The APNB version of what had happened seemed to deviate from the truth when it would have caused too many problems for the authorities. Deacon wore a satisfied smile on his face.

When the news report ended, Lucy turned off the television. At the same moment, there was heavy crash outside. Jett jumped up and went to investigate. Through the pelting rain, he could see broken pieces of Deacon's tree house lying on the ground. Shivering in the cold wind, he rubbed his arms and felt somewhat saddened by the sight. He turned around and walked back inside.

"What was it?" Deacon asked as Jett entered the room.

"You won't believe it. Your tree house, Deek! It just crashed to the ground!"

"Oh!" Deacon replied in dismay, feeling somewhat troubled by the incident.

"This is surreal! Where do we go from here?" Jett asked.

Lucy suddenly found her voice. "Isn't that obvious? You two must find the missing capsule and the Sacred Keeper! I don't usually like spiders, but this spider from Mars sounds quite intriguing, not to mention brave, trying to protect Onyx."

"Poor kid," Deacon replied. "Onyx gave his life doing what he believed was right. There's no greater sacrifice. He just wanted to help Earth's Crystals. Looks like it's up to us now, Jett!" He paused and then added thoughtfully, "Life is a journey. We should grab our destiny with both hands."

Recalling their times in the tree house, Jett smiled. "Well, Deek. Maybe we are meant to be defenders of Earth after all."

Deacon grinned at his grandfather. "Are you ready for another adventure, Grandpa?"

Grandpa shook his head in amazement. "Always, son."

While they were speaking, a strong current of air whipped through the trees, unleashing a series of discordant howls. The debris of daytime was carried across the night sky by a cold squall of wind. A discarded leaflet slapped wetly onto the Rainers' front door. Entitled "Life on Mars," the torn piece of paper announced a date, enticing all young space fanatics to stand by and be totally amazed.

To be continued …

Printed in the United States
By Bookmasters